D1460651

the further adventures of

SHERLOCK HOLMES

THE PEERLESS PEER

THE FURTHER ADVENTURES OF SHERLOCK HOLMES

THE PEERLESS PEER

JOHN H. WATSON, M.D.

EDITED BY
PHILIP JOSÉ FARMER

*American Agent For The Estates of Dr. Watson, Lord Greystoke,
David Copperfield, Martin Eden, And Don Quixote*

WITH AFTERWORD BY WIN SCOTT ECKERT

TITAN BOOKS

THE FURTHER ADVENTURES OF SHERLOCK HOLMES:
THE PEERLESS PEER
ISBN: 9780857681201

Published by
Titan Books
A division of Titan Publishing Group Ltd
144 Southwark St
London
SE1 0UP

First edition: June 2011
10 9 8 7 6 5 4 3 2 1

Names, places and incidents are either products of the author's
imagination or used fictitiously. Any resemblance to actual persons, living
or dead (except for satirical purposes), is entirely coincidental.

Visit our website:
www.titanbooks.com

What did you think of this book? We love to hear from our
readers. Please email us at: readerfeedback@titanemail.com,
or write to us at the above address. To receive advance information,
news, competitions, and exclusive Titan offers online, please register
as a member by clicking the 'sign up' button on our website:
www.titanbooks.com

A CIP catalogue record for this title is available from the British Library.

Printed in the USA.

Dedicated to Samuel Rosenberg, who has embroidered
for the world the greatest Doylie ever.

All the characters in this book are real;
any resemblance to fictional characters is
purely coincidental.

Foreword

A s everybody knows, Dr. Watson stored in a battered tin dispatch-box his manuscripts concerning the unpublished cases of Sherlock Holmes. This box was placed in the vaults of the bank of Cox and Co. at Charing Cross. Whatever hopes the world had that these papers would some day become public were destroyed when the bank was blasted into fragments during the bombings of World War II. It is said that Winston Churchill himself directed that the ruins be searched for the box but that no trace of it was found.

I am happy to report that this lack of success is no cause for regret. At a time and for reasons unknown, the box had been transferred to a little villa on the south slope of the Sussex Downs near the village of Fulworth. It was kept in a trunk in the attic of the villa. This, as everybody should know, was the residence of Holmes after he had retired. It is not known what eventually happened to the Greatest Detective. There is no record of his death. Even if there were, it would be disbelieved by the many who still think of him as a living person. This almost religious belief thrives though he would, if still alive, be one hundred and twenty years old at the date of writing this foreword.

Whatever happened to Holmes, his villa was sold in the late 1950s to the seventeenth Duke of Denver. The box, with some other objects, was removed to the ducal estate in Norfolk. His Grace had intended to wait until after his death before the papers would be allowed to be published. However, His Grace, though eighty-four years old now, feels that he may live to be a hundred. The world has waited far too long, and it is certainly ready for anything, no matter how shocking, that may be in Watson's narratives. The duke has given his consent to the publication of all but a few papers, and even these may see print if the descendants of certain people mentioned in them give their permission. Gratitude is due His Grace for this generous decision.

On hearing the good news, your editor communicated with the British agents handling the Watson papers and was fortunate enough to acquire the American Agency for them. The adventure at hand is the first to be released; others will follow from time to time.

Watson's holograph is obviously a first draft. A number of passages recording words actually uttered by the participants during this adventure are either crossed out or replaced with asterisks. The "peerless peer" of this tale is called "Greystoke," but on one occasion old habit broke through and Watson inadvertently wrote "Holdernesse." Watson left no note explaining why he had substituted one pseudotitle for another. He used "Holdernessee" in "The Adventure of the Priory School" to conceal the identity of Holmes' noble client. Holmes himself, in his reference to the nobleman in his "The Adventure of the Blanched Soldier," used the pseudotitle of "Greyminster."

It is your editor's guess that Watson decided on "Greystoke" in this narrative because the pseudotitle had been made world-famous by the novels based on the African exploits of the nephew of the man Watson had called "Holdernesse."

The adventure at hand is singular for many reasons. It reveals that Holmes was not allowed to stay in retirement after the events of "His Last Bow." We are made aware that Holmes made a second visit to Africa, going far beyond Khartoum (though not willingly), and so saved Great Britain from the greatest danger which has ever threatened it. We are given some illumination on the careers of the two greatest American aviators and spies in the early years of World War I. We learn that Watson was married for the fourth time, and the destruction of a civilization rivaling ancient Egypt is recorded for the first time. Holmes' contribution to apiology and how he used it to save himself and others is related herein. This narrative also describes how Holmes' genius at deduction enabled him to clear up a certain discrepancy that has puzzled the more discerning readers of the works of Greystoke's American biographer.

Some aspects of this discrepancy are revealed by Lord Greystoke himself in "Extracts from the Memoirs of Lord Greystoke," *Mother Was a Lovely Beast*, Philip José Farmer, editor, Chilton, October, 1974. However, this revelation is only a minor part of Watson's chronicle, one among many mysteries solved, and this account presents the mystery from a somewhat different viewpoint.

Your editor decided for these reasons to leave this explanation in this work. Besides, your editor would not dream of tampering with any part of the Sacred Writings.

– Philip José Farmer

One

It is with a light heart that I take up my pen to write these the last words in which I shall ever record the singular genius which distinguished my friend Sherlock Holmes. I realise that I once wrote something to that effect, though at that time my heart was as heavy as it could possibly be. This time I am certain that Holmes has retired for the last time. At least, he has sworn that he will no more go a-detecting. The case of the peerless peer has made him financially secure, and he foresees no more grave perils menacing our country now that out great enemy has been laid low. Moreover, he has sworn that never again will he set foot on any soil but that of his native land. Nor will he ever again get near an aircraft. The mere sight or sound of one freezes his blood.

The peculiar adventure which occupies these pages began on the second day of February, 1916. At this time I was, despite my age, serving on the staff of a military hospital in London. Zeppelins had made bombing raids over England for two nights previously, mainly in the Midlands. Though these were comparatively ineffective, seventy people had been killed, one hundred and thirteen injured, and a monetary damage of fifty-three thousand eight hundred and thirty-two pounds had been inflicted. These raids were the latest in a series starting the nineteenth of January. There was no panic, of course, but even stout British hearts were experiencing some uneasiness. There were rumours, no doubt originated by German agents, that the Kaiser intended to send across the channel a fleet of a thousand airships. I was discussing this rumour with my young friend, Dr. Fell, over a brandy in my quarters when a knock sounded on the door. I opened it to admit a messenger. He handed me a telegram which I wasted no time in reading.

"Great Scott!" I cried.

"What is it, my dear fellow?" Fell said, heaving himself from the chair. Even then, on war rations, he was putting on overly much weight.

"A summons to the F.O.," I said. "From Holmes. And I am on special leave."

"Sherlock?" said Fell.

"No, Mycroft," I replied. Minutes later, having packed my few belongings, I was being driven in a limousine toward the Foreign Office. An hour later, I entered the small austere room in which the massive Mycroft Holmes sat like a great spider spinning the web that ran throughout the British Empire and many alien lands. There were two others present, both of whom I knew. One was young Merrivale, a baronet's son, the brilliant aide to the head of the British Military Intelligence Department and soon to assume the chieftainship. He was also a qualified physician and had been one of my students when I was lecturing at Bart's. Mycroft claimed that Merrivale was capable of rivalling Holmes himself in the art of detection and would not be far behind Mycroft himself. Holmes' reply to this "needling" was that only practise revealed true promise.

I wondered what Merrivale was doing away from the War Office but had no opportunity to voice my question. The sight of the second person there startled me at the same time it delighted me. It had been over a year since I had seen that tall, gaunt figure with the greying hair and the unforgettable hawklike profile.

"My dear Holmes," I said. "I had thought that after the Von Bork affair…"

"The east wind has become appallingly cold, Watson," he said. "Duty recognises no age limits, and so I am called from my bees to serve our nation once more."

Looking even more grim, he added, "The Von Bork business is not over. I fear that we underestimated the fellow because we so easily captured him. He is not always taken with such facility. Our government erred grievously in permitting him to return to Germany with Von Herling. He should have faced a firing squad. A motor-car crash in Germany after his return almost did for us what we had failed to do, according to reports that have recently reached me. But, except for a permanent injury to his left eye, he has recovered.

"Mycroft tells me that Von Bork has done, and is doing, us inestimable damage. Our intelligence tells us that he is operating in Cairo, Egypt. But just where in Cairo and what disguise he has assumed is not known."

"The man is indeed dangerous," Mycroft said, reaching with a hand as ponderous as a grizzly's paw for his snuff-box. "It is no exaggeration to say that he is the most dangerous man in the world, as far as the Allies are concerned, anyway."

"Greater than Moriarty was?" Holmes said, his eyes lighting up.

"Much greater," replied Mycroft. He breathed in the snuff, sneezed, and wiped his jacket with a large red handkerchief. His watery grey eyes had lost their inward-turning look and burned as if they were searchlights probing the murkiness around a distant target.

"Von Bork has stolen the formula of a Hungarian refugee scientist employed by our government in Cairo. The scientist recently reported to his superiors the results of certain experiments he had been making on a certain type of bacillus peculiar to the land of the Pharaohs. He had discovered that this bacillus could be modified by chemical means to eat only sauerkraut. When a single bacillus was placed upon sauerkraut, it multiplied at a fantastic rate. It would become within sixty minutes a colony which would consume a pound of sauerkraut to its last molecule.

"You see the implications. The bacillus is what the scientists call a mutated type. After treatment with a certain chemical both its form and function are changed. Should we drop vials containing this mutation in Germany, or our agents directly introduce the germs, the entire nation would shortly become sauerkrautless. Both their food supply and their morale would be devastated.

"But Von Bork somehow got wind of this, stole the formula, destroyed the records and the chemicals with fire, and murdered the only man who knew how to mutate the bacillus.

"However, his foul deed was no sooner committed than detected. A tight cordon was thrown around Cairo, and we have reason to believe that Von Bork is hiding in the native quarter somewhere. We can't keep that net tight for long, my dear Sherlock, and that is why you must be gotten there quickly so you can track him down. England expects much from you, brother, and much, I am sure, will be given."

I turned to Holmes, who looked as shaken as I felt. "Surely, my dear fellow, we are not going to Cairo?"

"Surely indeed, Watson," he replied. "Who else could sniff out the Teutonic fox, who else could trap him? We are not so old that we cannot settle Von Bork's hash once and for all."

Holmes, I observed, was still in the habit of using Americanisms, I suppose because he had thrown himself so thoroughly into the role of an Irish-American while tracking down Von Bork in that adventure which I have titled "His Last Bow."

"Unless," he said, sneering, "you really feel that the old warhorse should not leave his comfortable pasture?"

"I am as good a man as I was a year and a half ago," I protested. "Have you ever known me to call it quits?"

He chuckled and patted my shoulder, a gesture so rare that my heart warmed.

"Good old Watson."

Mycroft called for cigars, and while we were lighting up, he said, "You two will leave tonight from a Royal Naval Air Service strip outside London. You will be flown by two stages to Cairo, by two different pilots, I should say. The fliers have been carefully selected because their cargo will be precious. The Huns may already know your destination. If they do, they will make desperate efforts to intercept you, but our fliers are the pick of the lot. They are fighter pilots, but they will be flying bombers. The first pilot, the man who'll take you under his wing tonight, is a young fellow. Actually, he is only seventeen, he lied to get into the service, but officially he is eighteen. He has downed seven enemy planes in two weeks and done yeoman service in landing our agents behind enemy lines. You may know of him, at least you knew his great-uncle."

He paused and said, "You remember, of course, the late Duke of Greystoke?"[1]

"I will never forget the size of the fee I collected from him," Holmes said, and he chuckled.

---

1 This is the line in which Watson inadvertently wrote "Holdernesse" but corrected it. *Editor.*

"Your pilot, Leftenant John Drummond, is the adopted son of the present Lord Greystoke," Mycroft continued.

"But wait!" I said. "Haven't I heard some rather strange things about Lord Greystoke? Doesn't he live in Africa?"

"Oh, yes, in darkest Africa," Mycroft said. "In a tree house, I believe."

"Lord Greystoke lives in a tree house?" I said.

"Ah, yes," Mycroft said. "Greystoke is living in a tree house with an ape. At least, that's one of the rumours I've heard."

"Lord Greystoke is living with an ape?" I said. "A female ape, I trust."

"Oh, yes," Mycroft said. "There's nothing queer about Lord Greystoke, you know."[2]

"But surely," I said, "this Lord Greystoke can't be the son of the old duke? Not the Lord Saltire, the duke's son, whom we rescued from kidnappers in the adventure of the Priory School?"

Holmes was suddenly as keen as an eagle that detects a lamb. He stooped toward his brother, saying, "Hasn't some connexion been made between His Grace and the hero of that fantastic novel by that American writer—what's-his-name?—Bayrows? Borrows? Isn't the Yank's protagonist modelled somewhat after Lord Greystoke? The book only came out in the States in June of 1914, I believe, and so very few copies have gotten here because of the blockade. But I've heard rumours of it. I believe that His Grace could sue for libel, slander, defamation of character and much else if he chose to notice the novel."

"I really don't know," Mycroft said. "I never read fiction."

---

2 Under normal circumstances your editor would delete this old joke. Doubtless the reader has heard it in one form or another. But it is Watson's narrative, and it is of historical importance. Now we know when and where the story originated.

"By the Lord Harry!" Merrivale said. "I do! I've read the book, a rattling good yarn but wild, wild. This heir to an English peerage is adopted by a female ape and raised with a tribe of wild and woolly..."

Mycroft slammed his palm against the top of the table, startling all of us and making me wonder what had caused this unheard-of violence from the usually phlegmatic Mycroft.

"Enough of this time-wasting chitchat about an unbalanced peer and an excessively imaginative Yankee writer!" he said. "The Empire is crumbling around our ears and we're talking as if we're in a pub and all's well with the world!"

He was right, of course, and all of us, including Holmes, I'm sure, felt abashed. But that conversation was not as irrelevant as we thought at the time.

An hour later, after receiving verbal instructions from Mycroft and Merrivale, we left in the limousine for the secret airstrip outside London.

Two

Our chauffeur drove off the highway onto a narrow dirt road which wound through a dense wood of oaks. After a half a mile, during which we passed many signs warning trespassers that this was military property, we were halted by a barbed wire gate across the road. Armed R.N.A.S. guards checked our documents and then waved us on. Ten minutes later, we emerged from the woods onto a very large meadow. At its northern end was a tall hill, the lower part of which gaped as if it had a mouth which was open with surprise. The surprise was that the opening was not to a cavern at all but to a hangar which had been hollowed out of the living rock of the hill. As we got out of the car, men pushed from the hangar a huge aeroplane, the wings of which were folded against the fuselage.

After that, events proceeded swiftly—too swiftly for me, I admit, and perhaps a trifle too swiftly for Holmes. After all, we had been born about a half century before the first aeroplane had flown. We were not sure that the motor-car, a recent invention from our viewpoint, was altogether a beneficial device. And here we were being conducted by a commodore toward the monstrously large aircraft. Within a few minutes, according to him, we would be within its fuselage and leaving the good earth behind and beneath us.

Even as we walked toward it, its biplanes were unfolded and locked into place. By the time we reached it, its propellors had been spun by mechanics and the two motors had caught fire. Thunder rolled from its rotaries, and flame spat from its exhausts.

Whatever Holmes' true feelings, and his skin was rather grey, he could not suppress his driving curiosity, his need to know all that was relevant. However, he had to shout at the commodore to be heard above the roar of the warming-up motors.

"The Admiralty ordered it to be outfitted for your use," the commodore said. His expression told us that he thought that we must be very special people indeed if this aeroplane was equipped just for us.

"It's the prototype model of the Handley Page 0/100," he shouted. "The first of the 'bloody paralyser of an aeroplane' the Admiralty ordered for the bombing of Germany. It has two 250-horsepower Rolls-Royce Eagle H motors, as you see. It has an enclosed crew cabin. The engine nacelles and the front part of the fuselage were armour-plated, but the armour has been removed to give the craft more speed."

"What?" Holmes yelled. "Removed?"

"Yes," the commodore said. "It shouldn't make any difference to you. You'll be in the cabin, and it was never armour-plated."

Holmes and I exchanged glances. The commodore continued, "Extra petrol tanks have been installed to give the craft extended range. These will be just forward of the cabin…"

"And if we crash?" Holmes said.

"Poof!" the commodore said, smiling, "No pain, my dear sir. If the smash doesn't kill you, the flaming petrol sears the lungs and causes instantaneous death. The only difficulty is in identifying the corpse. Charred, you know,"

We climbed up a short flight of wooden mobile steps and stepped into the cabin. The commodore closed the door, thus somewhat muting the roar. He pointed out the bunks that had been installed for our convenience and the W.C. This contained a small washbowl with a gravity-feed water tank and several thunder-mugs bolted to the deck.[3]

"The prototype can carry a four-man crew," the commodore said. "There is, as you have observed, a cockpit for the nose gunner, with the pilot in a cockpit directly behind him. There is a cockpit near the rear for another machine gunner, and there is a trap-door through which a machine gun may be pointed to cover the rear area under the plane. You are standing on the trap-door."

Holmes and I moved away, though not, I trust, with unseemly haste.

"We estimate that with its present load the craft can fly at approximately 85 miles per hour. Under ideal conditions, of course. We have decided to eliminate the normal armament of machine guns in order to lighten the load. In fact, to this end, all of the crew except the pilot and co-pilot are eliminated. The pilot, I believe, is bringing his personal arms: a dagger, several pistols, a carbine, and his specially mounted Spandau machine gun, a trophy, by the way, taken from a Fokker E-1 which Captain Wentworth downed when he dropped an ash-tray on the pilot's head. Wentworth has also brought in several cases of hand grenades and a case of Scotch whisky."

---

3 The good doctor probably intended to delete the references to sanitation in the final version of this adventure. At least, he always had been reticent to a Victorian degree in such references in all his previous chronicles. However, this was written in 1932, and Watson may have thought that the spirit of the times gave him more latitude in expression. *Editor.*

The door, or port, or whatever they call a door in the Royal Naval Air Service; opened, and a young man of medium height, but with very broad shoulders and a narrow waist, entered. He wore the uniform of the R.N.A.S. He was a handsome young man with eyes as steely grey and as magnetic as Holmes'. There was also something strange about them. If I had known how strange, I would have stepped off that plane at that very second. Holmes would have preceded me.

He shook hands with us and spoke a few words. I was astonished to hear a flat mid-western American accent. When Wentworth had disappeared on some errand toward the stern, Holmes asked the commodore, "Why wasn't a British pilot assigned to us? No doubt this Yank volunteer is quite capable, but really…"

"There is only one pilot who can match Wentworth's aerial genius. He is an American in the service of the Tsar. The Russians know him as Kentov, though that is not his real name. They refer to him with the honorific of *Chorniy Oryol*, the French call him *l'Aigle Noir* and the Germans are offering a hundred thousand marks for *Der Schwarz Adler*, dead or alive."

"Is he a Negro?" I said.

"No, the adjective refers to his sinister reputation," replied the commodore. "Kentov will take you on from Marseilles. Your mission is so important that we borrowed him from the Russians. Wentworth is being used only for the comparatively short haul since he is scheduled to carry out another mission soon. If you should crash, and survive, he would be able to guide you through enemy territory better than anyone we know of, excluding Kentov. Wentworth is an unparalleled master of disguise…"

"Really?" Holmes said, drawing himself up and frostily regarding the officer.

Aware that he had made a gaffe, the commodore changed the subject. He showed us how to don the bulky parachutes, which were to be kept stored under a bunk.

"What happened to young Drummond?" I asked him. "Lord Greystoke's adopted son? Wasn't he supposed to be our pilot?"

"Oh, he's in hospital," he said, smiling. "Nothing serious. Several broken ribs and clavicle, a liver that may be ruptured, a concussion and possible fracture of the skull. The landing gear of his craft collapsed as he was making a deadstick landing, and he slid into a brick wall. He sends his regards."

Captain Wentworth suddenly reappeared. Muttering to himself, he looked under our blankets and sheets and then under the bunks. Holmes said, "What is it, captain?"

Wentworth straightened up and looked at us with those strange grey eyes. "Thought I heard bats," he said. "Wings fluttering. Giant bats. But no sign of them."

He left the cabin then, heading down a narrow tunnel which had been specially installed so that the pilot could get into the cockpit without having to go outside the craft. His co-pilot, a Lieutenant Nelson, had been warming the motors. The commodore left a minute later after wishing us luck. He looked as if he thought we'd need it.

Presently, Wentworth phoned in to us and told us to lie down in the bunks or grab hold of something solid. We were getting ready to take off. We got into the bunks, and I stared at the ceiling while the plane slowly taxied to the starting point, the motors were "revved" up, and then it began to bump along the meadow. Within a short time its tail had lifted and we were suddenly aloft. Neither Holmes nor I could endure just lying there any more. We had to get up and look through the window in the door. The sight of the earth dropping away in the dusk, of houses, cows, horses and waggons, and brooks and then the Thames itself dwindling, dwindling caused us to be both uneasy and exhilarated.

Holmes was still grey, but I am certain that it was not fear of altitude that affected him. It was being completely dependent upon someone else, being not in control of the situation. On the ground Holmes was his own master. Here his life and limb were in the hands of two strangers, one of whom had already impressed us as being very strange. It also became obvious only too soon that Holmes, no matter how steely his nerves and how calm his digestion on earth, was subject to airsickness.

The plane flew on and on, crossing the channel in the dark, crossing the westerly and then the southwestern part of France. We landed on a strip lighted with flames. Holmes wanted to get out and stretch his legs but Wentworth forbade that.

"Who knows what's prowling around here, waiting to identify you and then to crouch and leap, destroying utterly?" he said.

After he had gone back to the cockpit, I said, "Holmes, don't you think he puts the possibility of spies in somewhat strange language? And didn't you smell Scotch on his breath? Should a pilot drink while flying?"

"Frankly," Holmes said, "I'm too sick to care," and he lay down outside the door to the W.C.

Midnight came with the great plane boring through the dark moonless atmosphere. Lt. Nelson crawled into his bunk with the cheery comment that we would be landing at a drome outside Marseilles by dawn. Holmes groaned. I bade the fellow, who seemed quite a decent sort, good-night. Presently I fell asleep, but I awoke some time later with a start. As an old veteran of Holmes' campaigns, however, I knew better than to reveal my awakened state. While I rolled over to one side as if I were doing it in my sleep, I watched through narrowed eyes.

A sound, or a vibration, or perhaps it was an old veteran's sixth sense, had awakened me. Across the aisle, illumined by the single bulb overhead, stood Lt. Nelson. His handsome youthful face bore an expression which the circumstances certainly did not seem to call for. He looked so malignant that my heart began thumping and perspiration poured out from me despite the cold outside the blankets. In his hand was a revolver, and when he lifted it my heart almost stopped. But he did not turn toward us. Instead he started toward the front end, toward the narrow tunnel leading to the pilot's cockpit.

Since his back was to me, I leaned over the edge of the bunk and reached down to get hold of Holmes. I had no need to warn him. Whatever his physical condition, he was still the same alert fox—an old fox, it is true, but still a fox. His hand reached up and touched mine, and within a few seconds he was out of the bunk and on his feet. In his one hand he held his trusty Webley, which he raised to point at Nelson's back, crying out to halt at the same time.

I do not know if he heard Holmes above the roar of the motors. If he did, he did not have time to consider it. There was a report, almost inaudible in the din, and Nelson fell back and slid a few feet along the floor backward. Blood gushed from his forehead.

The dim light fell on the face of Captain Wentworth, whose eyes seemed to blaze, though I am certain that was an optical illusion. The face was momentarily twisted, and then it smoothed out, and he stepped out into the light. I got down from the bunk and with Holmes approached him. Close to him, I could smell the heavy, though fragrant, odour of excellent Scotch on his breath.

Wentworth looked at the revolver in Holmes' hand, smiled, and said, "So—you are not overrated, Mr. Holmes! But I was waiting for him, I expected him to sneak in upon me while I should be concentrating on the instrument board. He thought he'd blow my a*s off!"

"He is, of course, a German spy," Holmes said. "But how did you determine that he was?"

"I suspect everybody," Wentworth replied. "I kept my eye on him, and when I saw him talking over the wireless, I listened in. It was too noisy to hear clearly, but he was talking in German. I caught several words, *schwanz* and *schweinhund.* Undoubtedly, he was informing the Imperial German Military Aviation Service of our location. If he didn't kill me, then we would be shot down. The Huns must be on their way to intercept us now."

This was alarming enough, but both Holmes and I were struck at the same time with a far more disturbing thought. Holmes as usual, was more quick in his reactions. He screamed, "Who's flying the plane?"

Wentworth smiled lazily and said, "Nobody. Don't worry. The controls are connected to a little device I invented last month. As long as the air is smooth, the plane will fly on an even keel all by itself."

He stiffened suddenly, cocked his head to one side, and said, "Do you hear it?"

"Great Scott, man!" I cried. "How could we hear anything above the infernal racket of those motors?"

"Cockroaches!" Wentworth bellowed. "Giant flying cockroaches! That evil scientist has released another horror upon the world!"

He whirled, and he was gone into the blackness of the tunnel.

Holmes and I stared at each other. Then Holmes said, "We are at the mercy of a madman, Watson. And there is nothing we can do until we have landed."

"We could parachute out," I said.

"I would prefer not to," Holmes said stiffly. "Besides, it somehow doesn't seem cricket. The pilots have no parachutes, you know. These two were provided only because we are civilians."

"I wasn't planning on asking Wentworth to ride down with me," I mumbled, somewhat ashamed of myself for saying this.

Holmes didn't hear me; once again his stomach was trying to reject contents that did not exist.

Three

Shortly after dawn, the German planes struck. These, as I was told later, were Fokker E-IIIs, single-seater monoplanes equipped with two Spandau machine guns. These were synchronised with the propellors to shoot bullets through the empty spaces between the whirling of the propellor blades.

Holmes was sitting on the floor, holding his head and groaning, and I was commiserating with him, though getting weary of his complaints, when the telephone bell rang. I removed the receiver from the box attached to the wall, or bulkhead, or whatever they call it. Wentworth's voice bellowed, "Put on the parachutes and hang on to something tight! Twelve ****ing Fokkers, a whole *staffel*, coming in at eleven o'clock!"

I misunderstood him. I said, "Yes, but what type of plane are they?"

"Fokkers!" he cried, adding, "No, no! My eyes played tricks on me. They're giant flying cockroaches! Each one is being ridden by a Prussian officer, helmeted and goggled and armed with a boarding cutlass!"

"What did you say?" I screamed into the phone, but it had been disconnected.

I told Holmes what Wentworth had said, and he forgot about being airsick, though he looked no better than before. We staggered out to the door and looked through its window.

The night was now brighter than day, the result of flares thrown out from the attacking aeroplanes. Their pilots intended to use the light to line up the sights of their machine guns on our helpless craft. Then, as if that were not bad enough, shells began exploding, some so near that our aeroplane shuddered and rocked under the impact of the blasts. Giant searchlights began playing about, some of them illuminating monoplanes with black crosses on their fuselages.

"Archy!" I exclaimed. "The French anti-aircraft guns are firing at the Huns! The fools! They could hit us just as well!"

Something flashed by. We lost sight of it, but a moment later we saw a fighter diving down toward us through the glare of the flares and the searchlights, ignoring the bursting shells around it. Two tiny red eyes flickered behind the propellor, but it was not until holes were suddenly punched in the fabric only a few feet from us that we realised that those were the muzzles of the machine guns. We dropped to the floor while the great plane rolled and dipped and rose and dropped and we were shot this way and that across the floor and against the bulkheads.

"We're doomed!" I cried to Holmes. "Get the parachutes on! He can't shoot back at the planes, and our plane is too slow and clumsy to get away!"

How wrong I was. And what a demon that madman was. He did things with that big lumbering aeroplane that I wouldn't have believed possible. Several times we were upside down and we only kept from being smashed, like mice shaken in a tin, by hanging on desperately to the bunkposts.

Once, Holmes, whose sense of hearing was somewhat keener than mine, said, "Watson, isn't that a*****e shooting a machine gun? How can he fly this plane, put it through such manoeuvres, and still operate a weapon which he must hold in both hands to use effectively?"

"I don't know," I confessed. At that moment both of us were dangling from the post, failing to fall only because of our tight grip. The plane was on its left side. Through the window beneath my feet I saw a German plane, smoke trailing from it, fall away. And then another followed it, becoming a ball of flame about a thousand feet or so from the ground.

The Handley Page righted itself, and I heard faint thumping noises overhead, followed by the chatter of a machine gun. Something exploded very near us and wreckage drifted by the window.

This shocked me, but even more shocking was the rapping on the window. This, to my astonishment, originated from a fist hammering on the door. I crawled over to it and stood up and looked through it. Upside down, staring at me through the isinglass, was Wentworth's face. His lips formed the words, "Open the door! Let me in!"

Numbly, I obeyed. A moment later, with an acrobatic skill that I still find incredible, he swung through the door. In one hand he held a Spandau with a rifle stock. A moment later, while I held on to his waist, he had closed the door and shut out the cold shrilling blast of wind.

"There they are!" he yelled, and he pointed the machine gun at a point just past Holmes, lying on the floor, and sent three short bursts past Holmes' ear.

Holmes said, "Really, old fellow…" Wentworth, raving, ran past him and a moment later we heard the chatter of the Spandau again.

"At least, he's back in the cockpit," Holmes said weakly. However, this was one of the times when Holmes was wrong. A moment later the captain was back. He opened the trap-door, poked the barrel of his weapon through, let loose a single burst, said, "Got you, you ****ing son of a *****!" closed the trap-door, and ran back toward the front.

Forty minutes later, the plane landed on a French military aerodrome outside of Marseilles. Its fuselage and wings were perforated with bullet holes in a hundred places, though fortunately no missiles had struck the petrol tanks. The French commander who inspected the plane pointed out that more of the holes were made by a gun firing from the inside than from guns firing from the outside.

"Damn right!" Wentworth said. "The cockroaches and their allies, the flying leopards, were crawling all over inside the plane! They almost got these two old men!"

A few minutes later a British medical officer arrived. Wentworth, after fiercely fighting six men, was subdued and put into a straitjacket and carried off in an ambulance.

Wentworth was not the only one raving. Holmes, his pale face twisted, his fists clenched, was cursing his brother Mycroft, young Merrivale, and everyone else who could possibly be responsible, excepting, of course, His Majesty.

We were taken to an office occupied by several French and British officers of very high rank. The highest, General Chatson-Dawes-Overleigh, said, "Yes, my dear Mr. Holmes, we realise that he sometimes has these hallucinatory fits. Becomes quite mad, to be frank. But he is the best pilot and also the best espionage agent we have, even if he is a Colonial, and he has done heroic work for us. He never hallucinates negatively, that is, he never harms his fellows—though he did shoot an Italian once, but the fellow *was* only a private and he *was* an Italian and it *was* an accident—and so we feel that we must permit him to work for us. We can't permit a word of his condition to get back to the civilian populace, of course, so I must require you to swear silence about the whole affair. Which you would have to do as a matter of course, and, of course, of patriotism. He'll be given a little rest cure, a drying-out, too, and then returned to duty. Britain sorely needs him."[4] Holmes raved some more, but he always was one to face realities and to govern himself accordingly. Even so, he could not resist making some sarcastic remarks about his life, which was also extremely valuable, being put into the care of a homicidal maniac. At last, cooling down, he said, "And the pilot who will fly us to Egypt? Is he also an irresponsible madman? Will we be in more danger from him than from the enemy?"

"He is said to be every bit as good a pilot as Wentworth," the general said. "He is an American…"

"Great Scott!" Holmes said. He groaned, and he added, "Why can't we have a pilot of good British stock, tried and true?"

"Both Wentworth and Kentov are of the best British stock," Overleigh said stiffly. "They're descended from some of the oldest and noblest stock of England. They have royal blood in them, as a matter of fact. But they happen to be Colonials. The man who will fly you from here has been working for His Majesty's cousin, the Tsar of all the Russias, as an espionage agent. The Tsar was kind enough to loan both him and one of the great Sikorski *Ilya Mourometz* Type V aeroplanes to us. Kentov flew here in it with a full crew, and it is ready to take off."

Holmes' face became even paler, and I felt every minute of my sixty-four years of age. We were not to get a moment's rest, and yet we had gone through an experience which would have sent many a youth to bed for several days.

---

4 This mad, but usually functioning, American must surely be the great aviator and espionage agent who, after transferring to the U.S. forces in 1917, was known under the code name of G–8. While in the British service, he apparently went under the name of Wentworth, his half-brother's surname. For the true names of G–8, the Spider, and the Shadow, see my *Doc Savage: His Apocalyptic Life,* Bantam, 1975. *Editor.*

Four

General Overleigh himself conducted us to the colossal Russian aeroplane. As we approached it, he described certain features in answer to Holmes' questions.

"So far, the only four-engined heavier-than-air craft in the world has been built by the Russians," he said. "Much to the shame of the British. The first one was built, and flown, in 1913. This, as you can see, is a biplane, fitted with wheels and a ski undercarriage. It has four 150-horsepower Sunbeam water-cooled Vee-type engines. The Sunbeam, unfortunately, leaves much to be desired."

"I would rather not have known that," I murmured. The sudden ashen hue of Holmes' face indicated that his reactions were similar to mine.

"Its wing span is 97 feet 9½ inches; the craft's length is 56 feet 1 inch; its height is 15 feet 5 and seven-eighths inches. Its maximum speed is 75 miles per hour; its operational ceiling is 9,843 feet. And its endurance is five hours—under ideal conditions. It carries a crew of five, though it can carry more. The rear fuselage is fitted with compartments for sleeping and eating."

Overleigh shook hands with us after he had handed us over to a Lieutenant Obrenov. The young officer led us up the steps into the fuselage and to the rear, where he showed us our compartment. Holmes chatted away with him in Russian, of which he had gained a certain mastery during his experience in Odessa with the Trepoff case. Holmes' insistence on speaking Russian seemed to annoy the officer somewhat, since, like all upper-class people of his country, he preferred to use French. But he was courteous, and after making sure we were comfortable, he bowed himself out. Certainly, we had little to complain about except possibly the size of the cabin. It had been prepared especially for us, had two swing-down beds, a thick rug which Holmes said was a genuine Persian, oil paintings on the walls which Holmes said were genuine Maleviches (I thought they were artistic nonsense), two comfortable chairs bolted to the deck, and a sideboard also bolted to the deck and holding alcoholic beverages. In one corner was a tiny cubicle containing all the furniture and necessities that one finds in a W.C.

Holmes and I lit up the fine Cuban cigars we found in a humidor and poured out some Scotch whisky, Duggan's Dew of Kirkintilloch, I believe. Suddenly, both of us leaped into the air, spilling our drinks over our cuffs. Seemingly from nowhere, a tall figure had silently appeared. How he had done it, I do not know, since the door had been closed and under observation at all times by one or both of us.

Holmes groaned and said, under his breath, "Not another madman?"

The fellow certainly looked eccentric. He wore the uniform of a colonel of the Imperial Russian Air Service, but he also wore a long black opera cloak and a big black slouch hat. From under its floppy brim burned two of the most magnetic and fear-inspiring eyes I have ever seen. My attention, however, was somewhat diverted from these by the size and the aquilinity of the nose beneath them. It could have belonged to Cyrano de Bergerac.[5]

I found that I had to sit down to catch my breath. The fellow introduced himself, in an Oxford accent, as Colonel Kentov. He had a surprisingly pleasant voice, deep, rich, and shot with authority. It was also heavily laced with Bourbon.

"Are you all right?" he said.

"I think so," I said. "You gave me quite a start. A cloud seemed to pass over my mind. But I'm fine now, thank you."

"I must go forward now," he said, "but I've assigned a crew member, a tail gunner now but once a butler, to serve you. Just ring that bell beside you if you need him."

And he was gone, though this time he opened the door. At least, I think he did.

"I fear, my dear fellow, that we are in for another trying time," Holmes said.

Actually, the voyage seemed quite pleasant once one got used to the roar of the four motors and the nerve-shaking jack-out-of-the-box appearances of Kentov. The trip was to take approximately twenty-eight hours if all went well. The only time we landed was to refuel. About every four and a half hours, we put down at a hastily constructed landing strip to which petrol and supplies had been rushed by ship, air, or camel some days before. With the Mediterranean Sea on our left and the shores of North Africa below us, we sped toward Cairo at an amazing average speed of 70.3 miles

---

5 The description of this man certainly fits that of a notable crime fighter operating out of Manhattan in the '30's through the '40's. If he is who I think he is, then one of his many aliases was Lamont Cranston. *Editor.*

per hour, according to our commander. While we sipped various liquors or liqueurs and smoked Havanas, we read to pass the time. Holmes commented several times that he could use a little cocaine to relieve the tedium, but I believe that he said that just to needle me. Holmes had brought along a work of his own authorship, the privately printed *Practical Handbook of Bee Culture, With Some Observations Upon the Segregation of the Queen*. He had often urged me to read the results of his experience with his Sussex bees and so I now acceded to his urgings, mainly because all the other books available were in Russian.

I found it more interesting than I had expected, and I told Holmes so. This seemed to please him, though he had affected an air of indifference to my reaction before then.

"The techniques and tricks of apiculture are intriguing and complex enough," he said. "But I was called away from a project which goes far beyond anything any apiculturist—scientist or not—has attempted. It is my theory that bees have a language and that they communicate such important information as the location of new clover, the approach of enemies, and so forth, by means of symbolic dancing. I was investigating this with a view to turning theory into fact when I got Mycroft's wire."

I sat up so suddenly that the ash dropped off my cigar onto my lap, and I was busy for a moment brushing off the coals before they burned a hole in my trousers. "Really, Holmes," I said, "you are surely pulling my leg! Bees have a language? Next you'll be telling me they compose sonnets in honour of their queen's inauguration! Or perhaps epitases when she gets married!"

"Epitases?" he said, regarding me scornfully. "You mean epithalamiums, you blockhead! I suggest you use moderation while drinking the national beverage of Russia. Yes, Watson, bees do communicate, though not in the manner which *Homo sapiens* uses."[6]

"Perhaps you'd care to explain just what..." I said, but I was interrupted by that sudden vagueness of mind which signalled the appearance of our commander. I always jumped and my heart beat hard when the cloud dissolved and I realised that Kentov was standing before me. My only consolation was that Holmes was just as startled.

"Confound it, man!" Holmes said, his face red. "Couldn't you behave like a civilised being for once and knock before entering? Or don't Americans have such customs?"

This, of course, was sheer sarcasm, since Holmes had been to the States several times.

"We are only two hours from Cairo," Kentov said, ignoring Holmes' remarks. "But I have just learned from the wireless station in Cairo that a storm of severe proportions is approaching us from the north. We may be blown somewhat off our course. Also, our spies at Cos, in Turkey, report that a Zeppelin left there yesterday. They believe that it intends to pick up Von Bork. Somehow, he's slipped out past the cordon and is waiting in the desert for the airship."

Holmes, gasping and sputtering, said, "If this execrable voyage turns out to be for nothing... If I was forced to endure that madman's dangerous antics only to have...!"

Suddenly, the colonel was gone. Holmes regained his normal colour and composure, and he said, "Do you know, Watson, I believe I know that man! Or, at least, his parents. I've been studying him at every opportunity, and though he is doubtless a master at dissimulation, that nose is false, he has a certain bone structure and a certain trait of walking, of turning his head, which leads me to believe..."

---

6 For the first time we learn that Holmes anticipated the discovery of the Austrian scientist, von Frisch, by many decades. *Editor.*

At that moment the telephone rang. Since I was closest to the instrument, I answered it. Our commander's voice said, "Batten down all loose objects and tie yourself in to your beds. We are in for a hell of a storm, the worst of this century, if the weather reports are accurate."

For once, the meteorologists had not exaggerated. The next three hours were terrible. The giant aeroplane was tossed about as if it were a sheet of writing paper. The electric lamps on the walls flickered again and again and finally went out, leaving us in darkness. Holmes groaned and moaned and finally tried to crawl to the W.C. Unfortunately, the craft was bucking up and down like a wild horse and rolling and yawing like a rowboat caught in a rapids. Holmes managed to get back to his bed without breaking any bones but, I regret to say, proceeded to get rid of all the vodka and brandy (a combination itself not conducive to good digestion, I believe), beef stroganoff, cabbage soup, and black bread on which we had dined earlier. Even more regrettably, he leaned over the edge of the bed to perform this undeniable function, and though I did not get all of it, I did get too much. I did not have the heart to reprimand him. Besides, he would have killed me, or at least attempted to do so, if I had made any reproaches. His mood was not of the best.

Finally, I heard his voice, weak though it was, saying, "Watson, promise me one thing."

"What is that, Holmes?"

"Swear to me that once we've set foot on land you'll shoot me through the head if ever I show the slightest inclination to board a flying vehicle again. I don't think there's much danger of that, but even if His Majesty himself should plead with me to get into an aeroplane, or anything that flies, dirigible, balloon, anything, you will mercifully tender euthanasia of some sort. Promise me."

I thought I was safe in promising. For one thing, I felt almost as strongly as he did about it.

At that moment, the door to our cabin opened, and our attendant, Ivan, appeared with a small electric lamp in his hand. He exchanged some excited words in Russian with Holmes and then left, leaving the lamp behind. Holmes crawled down from the bunk, saying, "We've orders to abandon ship, Watson. We've been blown far south of Cairo and will be out of petrol in half an hour. We'll have to jump then, like it or not. Ivan says that the colonel has looked for a safe landing place, but he can't even see the ground. The air's filled with sand; visibility is nil; the sand is getting into the bearings of the engines and pitting the windshield. So, my dear old friend, we must don the parachutes."

My heart warmed at being addressed so fondly, though my emotion was somewhat tempered in the next few minutes while we were assisting each other in strapping on the equipment. Holmes said, "You have an abominable effluvia about you, Watson," and I replied, testily, I must admit, "You stink like the W.C. in an East End pub yourself, my dear Holmes. Besides, any odour emanating from me has originated from, or in, you. Surely you are aware of that."

Holmes muttered something about the direction upwards, and I was about to ask him to clarify his comment when Ivan appeared again. This time he carried weapons which he distributed among the three of us. I was handed a cavalry sabre, a stiletto, a knout (which I discarded), and a revolver of some unknown make but of .50 calibre. Holmes was given a cutlass, a carbine, a belt full of ammunition, and a coil of rope at one end of which were grappling hooks. Ivan kept for himself another cutlass, two hand grenades dangling by their pins from his belt, and a dagger in his teeth.

We walked (rolled, rather) to the door, where three others stood, also fully, perhaps even over-, armed. There was a window further forward, and so Holmes and I went to it after a while to observe the storm. We could see little except clouds of dust for a few minutes and then the dust was suddenly gone. A heavy rain succeeded it, though the wind buffeted us as strongly as before. There was also much lightning, some of it exploding loudly close by.

A moment later Ivan joined us, pulling at Holmes' arm and shouting something in Russian.

Holmes answered him and turning to me said, "Kentov has sighted a Zeppelin!"

"Great Scott!" I cried. "Surely it must be the one sent to pick up Von Bork! It, too, has been caught by the storm!"

"An elementary deduction," Holmes said. But he seemed pleased about something. I surmised that he was happy because Von Bork had either missed the airship or, if he was in it, was in as perilous a plight as we. I failed to see any humour in the situation.

Holmes lost his grin several minutes later when we were informed that we were going to attack the Zeppelin.

"In this storm?" I said. "Why, the colonel can't even keep us at the same altitude or attitude from one second to the next."

"The man's a maniac!" Holmes shouted.

Just how mad, we were shortly to discover. Presently the great airship hove into view, painted silver above and black below to conceal it from search lights, the large designation L9[7] on its side, the control car in front, its pusher propellor spinning, the propellors on the front and rear of the two midships and one aft engine-gondolas spinning, the whole looking quite monstrous and sinister and yet beautiful.

---

7 According to German official records the L9 was burned on September 16, 1916, in the *Fuhlsbüttel* shed because of a fire in the L6. Either Watson was in error or the Germans deliberately falsified the records in order to conceal the secret attempt to rescue Von Bork. At the time this adventure occurred, the L9 was supposed to be in action in Europe and its commander was Kapitän-leutnant d. R. Prölss. *Editor.*

The airship was bobbing and rolling and yawing like a toy boat afloat on a Scottish salmon stream. Its crew had to be airsick and they had to have their hands full just to keep from being pitched out of their vessel. This was heartening to some degree, since none of us on the aeroplane, except possibly Kentov, were in any state remotely resembling good health or aggression.

Ivan mumbled something, and Holmes said, "He says that if the storm keeps up the airship will soon break up. Let us hope it does and so spares us aerial combat."

But the Zeppelin, though it did seem to be somewhat out of line, its frame slightly twisted, held together. Meanwhile, our four-engined colossus, so small compared to the airship, swept around to the vessel's stern. It was a ragged approach what with the constantly buffeting blasts, but the wonder was that it was accomplished at all.

"What's the fool doing?" Holmes said, and he spoke again to Ivan. Lightning rolled up the heavens then, and I saw that his face was a ghastly blue-grey.

"This Yank is madder than the other!" he said. "He's going to try to land on top of the Zeppelin!"

"How could he do that?" I gasped.

"How would I know what techniques he'll use, you dunce!" he shouted. "Who cares? Whatever he does, the plane will fall off the ship, probably break its wings, and we'll fall to our deaths!"

"We can jump *now*!" I shouted.

"What? Desert?" he cried. "Watson, we are British!"

"It was only a suggestion," I said. "Forgive me. Of course, we will stick it out. No Slav is going to say that we English lack courage."

Ivan spoke again, and Holmes relayed his intelligence. "He says that the colonel, who is probably the greatest flier in the world, even if he is a Yank, will come up over the stern of the Zeppelin and stall it just above the top machine-gun platform. As soon as the plane stops, we are to open the door and leap out. If we miss our footing or fall down, we can always use the parachutes. Kentov insisted on bringing them along over the protests of the Imperial Russian General Staff—they should live so long. We will go down the ladder from the platform and board the ship. Kentov's final words, his last orders before we leave the plane are…"

He hesitated, and I said, "Yes, Holmes?"

"Kill! Kill! Kill!"

"Good heavens!" I said. "How barbaric!"

"Yes," he answered. "But one has to excuse him. He is obviously not sane."

Five

ollowing orders communicated through Obrenov, we lay down on the deck and grabbed whatever was solid and anchored in a world soon to become all too fluid and foundationless. The plane dived and we slid forward and then it rose sharply upward and we slid backward and then its nose suddenly lifted up, the roaring of the four engines becoming much more highly pitched, and suddenly we were pressed against the floor. And then the pressure was gone.

Slowly, but far too swiftly for me, the deck tilted to the left. This was in accordance with Kentov's plans. He had stalled it with its longitudinal axis, or centre-line, a little to the left, of the airship's centre-line. Its weight would thus cause the airship on whose back it rode to roll to the left.

For a second, I did not realise what was happening. To be quite frank, I was scared out of my wits, numb with terror. I would never allow Holmes to see this, and so I overcame my frozen state, though not the stiffness and slowness due to my age and recent hardships. I got up and stumbled out through the door, the parachute banging the upper parts of the back of my thighs and feeling as if it were made of lead, and sprawled out onto the small part of the platform left to me. I grabbed for the lowest end of an upright pipe forming the enclosure about the platform. The hatch had already been opened and Kentov was inside the airship. I could hear the booming of several guns. It was comparatively silent now, since Kentov had cut the engines just before the stalling. Nevertheless, the wind was howling and under it one could hear the creaking of the girders of the ship's structure as it bent under the varying pressures. My ears hurt abominably because the airship was dropping swiftly under the weight of the giant aeroplane. The aeroplane was also making its own unmistakable noises, groaning, as its structure bent, tearing the cotton fabric of the ship's covering as it slipped more and more to the left, then there was a loud ripping, and the ship beneath me rolled swiftly back, relieved of the enormous weight of the aeroplane. At the same time the Zeppelin soared aloft, and the two motions, the rolling and the levitation, almost tore me loose from my hold.

When the dirigible had ceased its major oscillations, the Russians rose and one by one disappeared into the well. Holmes and I worked our way across, passed the pedestals of the two quilt-swathed eight-millimetre Maxim machine guns, and descended the ladder. Just before I was all the way into the hatch, I looked across the back of the great beast that we were invading. I would have been shocked if I had not been so numb. The wheels and the ski undercarriage of the plane had ripped open a great wound along the thin skin of the vessel. Encountering the duralumin girders and rings of the framework, it had torn some apart and then its landing gear had itself been ripped off. The propellors, though no longer turning, had also done extensive damage. I wondered if the framework of the ship, the skeleton of the beast, as it were, might not have suffered so great a blow it would collapse and carry all of us down to our death.

I also had a second's admiration for the skill, no, the genius, of the pilot who had landed us.

And then I descended into the vast complex spider-web of the ship's hull with its rings and girders and bulging hydrogen-filled gas cells and ballast sacks of water. I emerged at the keel of the ship, on the foot-wide catwalk that ran the length of the ship between triangular girders. It had been a nightmare before then; after that it became a nightmare having a nightmare. I remember dodging along, clinging to girders, swinging out and climbing around to avoid the fire of the German sailors in the bow. I remember Lt. Obrenov falling with fatal bullet wounds after sticking two Germans with his sabre (there was no room to swing it and so use the edge as regulations required).

I remember others falling, some managing to retain their grip and so avoiding the fall through the fabric of the cover and into the abyss below. I remember Holmes hiding behind a gas cell and firing away at the Germans who were afraid of firing back and perhaps setting the hydrogen aflame.[8]

Most of all I remember the slouch-hatted cloaked form of Kentov leaping about, swinging from girders and brace wires, bouncing from a beam onto a great gas cell and back again, flitting like a phantom of the opera through the maze, firing, two huge .45 automatic pistols (not at the same time, of course, otherwise he would have lost his grip). German after German cried out or fled while the maniac cackled with a blood-chilling laugh between the booming of the huge guns. But though he was worth a squadron in himself, his men died one by one. And so the inevitable happened.

Perhaps it was a ricocheting bullet or perhaps he slipped. I do not know. All of a sudden he was falling off a girder, through a web of

---

8 There was actually no danger of fire since phosphorus-coated bullets were not being used. Apparently, the grenades, which might have set off the hydrogen, were not used. *Editor.*

wires, miraculously missing them, falling backward, now in each hand a thundering flame-spitting .45, killing two sailors as he fell, laughing loudly even as he broke through the cotton fabric and disappeared into the dark rain over Africa.

Since he was wearing a parachute, he may have survived. I never heard of him again, though.

Presently the Germans approached cautiously, having heard Holmes and me call out that we surrendered. (We were out of ammunition and too nerveless even to lift a sabre.) We stood on the catwalk with our hands up, two tired beaten old men. Yet it was our finest hour. Nothing could ever rob us of the pleasure of seeing Von Bork's face when he recognised us. If the shock had been slightly more intense, he would have dropped dead from a heart attack.

Six

A few minutes later, we had climbed down the ladder from the hull to the control gondola under the fore part of the airship. Behind us, raving, restrained by a petty officer and the executive officer, *Oberleutnant zur See* Heinrich Tring, came Von Bork. He had ordered us thrown overboard then and there, but Tring, a decent fellow, had refused to obey his orders. We were introduced to the commander, *Kapitänleutnant* Victor Reich.[9] He was also a decent fellow, openly admiring our feat of landing and boarding his ship even though it and his crew had suffered terribly. He rejected Von Bork's suggestion that we should be shot as spies since we were in civilian clothes and on a Russian warcraft. He knew of us, of course, and he would have nothing to do with a summary execution of the great Holmes and his colleague. After hearing our story, he made

---

9 The records of the Imperial German Navy have been combed without success in a search for identification of the L9 and the crew members mentioned by Watson. Could it be that the ship and crew were secret agents also, that the L9 was a "phantom" ship, that it carried out certain missions which the German concealed from all but the highest? Or were there records, but these are still in closed files or were destroyed for one reason or another? *Editor.*

sure of our comfort. However, he refused to let Holmes smoke, cast his tobacco overboard then and there, in fact, and this made Holmes suffer. He had gone through so much that he desperately needed a pipeful of shag.

"It is fortunate that the storm is breaking up," Reich said in excellent English. "Otherwise, the ship would soon break up. Three of our motors are not operating. The clutch to the port motor has overheated, the water in the radiator of a motor in the starboard mid-car has boiled out, and something struck the propellor of the control car and shattered it. We are so far south that even if we could operate at one hundred percent efficiency, we would be out of petrol somewhere over Egypt on the return trip. Moreover, the controls to the elevators have been damaged. All we can do at present is drift with the wind and hope for the best."

The days and nights that followed were full of suffering and anxiety. Seven of the crew had been killed during the fight, leaving only six to man the vessel. This alone was enough to make a voyage back to Turkey or Palestine impossible. Reich told us that he had received a radio message ordering him to get to the German forces in East Africa under Von Lettow-Vorbeck. There he was to burn the Zeppelin and join the forces. This, of course, was not all the message. Surely something must have been said about getting Von Bork back to Germany, since he had the formula for mutating and culturing the "sauerkraut bacilli."

When we were alone in the port mid-gondola, where we were kept during part of the voyage, Holmes commented on what he called the "SB."

"We must get possession of the formula, Watson," he said. "I did not tell you, but before you arrived at Mycroft's office I was informed that the SB is a two-edged weapon. It can be mutated to eat other foods. Imagine what would happen to our food supply, not to mention the blow to our morale, if the SB were changed to eat boiled meat? Or cabbage? Or potatoes?"

"Great Scott!" I said, and then, in a whisper, "It could be worse, Holmes, far worse. What if the Germans dropped an SB over England which devoured stout and ale? Or think of how the spirits of our valiant Scots would sink if their whisky supply vanished before their eyes?"

Von Bork had been impressed into service but, being as untrained as we, was not of much use. Also, his injured left eye handicapped him as much as our age did us. It was very bloodshot and failed to coordinate with its partner. My professional opinion was that it was totally without sight. The other eye was healthy enough. It glared every time it lighted upon us. Its fires reflected the raging hatred in his heart, the lust to murder us.

However, the airship was in such straits that no one had much time or inclination to think about anything except survival. Some of the motors were still operating, thus enabling some kind of control. As long as we went south, with the wind behind us, we made headway. But due to the jammed elevators, the nose of the ship was downward and the tail was up. The L9 flew at roughly five degrees to the horizontal for some time. Reich put everybody to work, including us, since we had volunteered, at carrying indispensable equipment to the rear to help weigh it down. Anything that was dispensable, and there was not much, went overboard. In addition, much water ballast in the front was discharged.

Below us the sands of Sudan reeled by, while the sun flamed in a cloudless blue. Its fiery breath heated the hydrogen in the cells, and great amounts hissed out from the automatic valves. The hot wind blew into the hull through the great hole made by the aeroplane when it had stalled into a landing on its top. The heat, of course, made the hydrogen expand, thus causing the ship to rise despite the loss of gas from the valves. At night, the air cooled very swiftly, and the ship dropped swiftly, too swiftly for the peace of mind of its passengers. During the day the updrafts of heat from the sands made the vessel buck and kick. All of us aboard got sick during these times.

By working like Herculeses despite all handicaps, the crew managed to get all the motors going again. On the fifth day, the elevator controls were fixed. Her hull was still twisted, and this, with the huge gap in the surface covering, made her aerodynamically unstable. At least, that was how Reich explained it to us. He, by the way, was not at all reticent in telling us about the vessel itself though he would not tell us our exact location. Perhaps this was because he wanted to make sure that we would not somehow get to the radio and send a message to the British in East Africa.

The flat desert gave way to rugged mountains. More ballast was dropped, and the L9 just barely avoided scraping some of the peaks. Night came with its cooling effects, and the ship dropped. The mountains were lower at this point, fortunately for us.

Two days later, as we lay sweltering on the catwalk that ran along the keel, Holmes said, "I estimate that we are now somewhere over British East Africa, somewhere in the vicinity of Lake Victoria. It is evident that we will never get to Mahenge or indeed anywhere in German East Africa. The ship has lost too much hydrogen. I have overheard some guarded comments to this effect by Reich and Tring. They think we'll crash sometime tonight. Instead of seeking out the nearest British authorities and surrendering, as anyone with good sense would, they are determined to cross our territory to German territory. Do you know how many miles of veldt and jungle and swamp swarming with lions, rhinoceri, vipers; savages, malaria, dengue, and God knows what else we will have to walk? Attempt to walk, rather?"

"Perhaps we can slip away some night?"

"And then what will we do?" he said bitterly. "Watson, you and I know the jungles of London well and are quite fitted to conduct our safaris through them. But here... no, Watson, any black child of eight is more competent, far more so, to survive in these wilds."

"You don't paint a very good picture," I said grimly.

"Though I am descended from the Vernets, the great French artists," he said, "I myself have little ability at painting pretty pictures."

He chuckled then, and I was heartened by this example of pawky humour, feeble though it was. Holmes would never quit; his indomitable English spirit might be defeated, but it would go down fighting. And I would be at his side. And was it not after all better to die with one's boots on while one still had some vigour than when one was old and crippled and sick and perhaps an idiot drooling and doing all sorts of pitiful, sickening things?

That evening preparations were made to abandon the ship. Ballast water was put in every portable container, the food supply was stored in sacks made from the cotton fabric ripped off the hull, and we waited. Sometime after midnight, the end came. It was fortunately a cloudless night with a moon bright enough for us to see, if not too sharply, the terrain beneath. This was a jungle up in the mountains, which were not at a great elevation. The ship was steered down a winding valley through which a stream ran silvery. Then, abruptly, we had to rise, and we could not do it.

We were in the control car when the hillside loomed before us. Reich gave the order and we threw our supplies out, thus lightening the load and giving us a few more seconds of grace. We two prisoners were courteously allowed to drop out first. Reich did this because the ship would rise as the crew members left, and he wanted us to be closest to the ground, We were old and not so agile, and he thought that we needed all the advantages we could get.

He was right. Even though Holmes and I fell into some bushes which eased our descent, we were still bruised and, shaken up. We scrambled out, however, and made our way through the growth toward the supplies. The ship passed over us, sliding its great shadow like a cloak, and then it struck something. The whirring propellors were snapped off, the cars crumpled and came loose with a nerve-scraping sound, the ship lifted again with the weight of the cars gone, and it drifted out of sight. But its career was about over. A few minutes later, it exploded. Reich had left several time-bombs next to some gas cells.

The flames were very bright and very hot, outlining the dark skeleton of its framework. Birds flew up and around it. No doubt they and the beasts of the jungle were making a loud racket, but the roar of the flames drowned them out.

By their light we could see back down the hill, though not very far. We struggled through the heavy vegetation, hoping to get to the supplies before the others. We had agreed to take as much food and water as we could carry and set off by ourselves, if we got the chance. Surely, we reasoned, there must be some native village nearby, and once there we would ask for guidance to the nearest British post.

By pure luck, we came across a pile of food and some bottles of water. Holmes said, "Dame Fortune is with us, Watson!" but his chuckle died the next moment when Von Bork stepped out of the bushes. In his hand was a Luger automatic and in his one eye was the determination to use that before the others arrived. He could claim, of course, that we were fleeing or had attacked him and that he was forced to shoot us.

"Die, you pig-dogs!" he snarled, and he raised the gun. "Before you do, though, know that I have the formula on me and that I will get it to the Fatherland and it will doom you English swine and the French swine and the Italian swine. The bacilli can be adapted to eat Yorkshire pudding and snails and spaghetti, anything that is edible! The beauty of it is that it's specific, and unless it's mutated to eat sauerkraut, it will starve rather than do so!"

We drew ourselves up, prepared to die as British men should. Holmes muttered out of the corner of his mouth, "Jump to one side, Watson, and then we'll rush him! You take his blind side! Perhaps one of us can get to him!"

This was a noble plan, though I didn't know what I could do even if I got hold of Von Bork.

After all, he was a young man and had a splendid physique.

At that moment there was a crashing in the bushes, Reich's loud voice commanding Von Bork not to shoot, and the commander, tears streaming from his face, stumbled into the little clearing. Behind him came others. Von Bork said, "I was merely holding them until you got here."

Reich, I must add, was not weeping because of any danger to us. The fate of his airship had dealt him a terrible blow; he loved his vessel and to see it die was to him comparable to seeing his wife die. Perhaps it had even more impact, since, as I later found out, he was on the verge of a divorce.

Though he had saved us, he knew that we were ready to skip out at the first chance. He kept a close eye on us, though it was not as close as Von Bork's. Nevertheless, he allowed us to retreat behind bushes to attend to our comforts. And so, three days later, we strolled on away.

"Well, Watson," Holmes said, as we sat panting under a tree several hours later, "we have given them the slip. But we have no water and no food except these pieces of mouldy biscuit in our pockets. At this moment I would trade them for a handful of shag."

We went to sleep finally and slept like the two old and exhausted men we were. I awoke several times, I think because of insects crawling over my face, but I always went back to sleep quickly. About eight in the morning, the light and the uproar of jungle life awoke us. I was the first to see the cobra slipping through the tall growths toward us. I got quickly, though unsteadily and painfully, to my feet. Holmes saw the reptile then and started to get up. The snake raised its upper part, its hood swelled, and it swayed as it turned its head this way and that.

"Steady, Watson!" Holmes said, though the advice would better have been given to himself. He was much closer to the cobra, within striking range, in fact, and he was shaking more violently than I. He could not be blamed for this, of course. He was in a more shakeable situation.

"I knew we should have brought along that flask of brandy," I said. "We have absolutely nothing for snakebite."

"No time for reproaches, you imbecile!" Holmes said. "Besides, what kind of medical man are you? It's sheer superstitious nonsense that alcohol helps prevent the effects of venom."

"Really, Holmes," I said. He had been getting so irascible lately, so insulting. Part of this could be excused, since he became very nervous without the solace of tobacco. Even so, I thought...

The thought was never finished. The cobra struck, and Holmes and I both jumped, yelling at the same time.

Something hissed through the air. The cobra was knocked aside by the impact of a missile, and it writhed dying on the ground. An arrow transfixed it just back of the head.

"Steady, Watson!" Holmes said. "We are saved, but the savage who shot that may have preserved us only so he'll have fresher meat for his pot!"

Suddenly, we leaped into the air again, uttering a frightened scream.

Seemingly out of the air, a man had appeared before us.

My heart was beating too hard and my breath was coming too swiftly for me to say anything for a moment.

Holmes recovered first.

He said, "Lord Greystoke, I presume?"

Seven

He seemed to be a giant, though actually he was only about three inches taller than Holmes. His bones were large, extraordinarily so, and though he was muscular, the muscles were not the knots of the professional strong man. Where a wrestler or weight lifter recalls a gorilla, he resembled a leopard. The face was handsome and striking. His hair was chopped off at the base of the neck, apparently by use of the huge hunting knife in the scabbard suspended by an antelope-skin belt just above the leopard-skin loincloth. The hair was as black as an Arab's, as was the bronzed skin which was criss-crossed with scars. His eyes were large and dark grey and had about them something both feral and remote. His nose was straight, his upper lip was short, and his chin was square and clefted.

He held in one hand a short thick bow of some wood and carried on his back a quiver with a dozen more arrows.

So this is Lord Greystoke, I thought. Yes, his features are enough like those of the ten-year-old Lord Saltire we rescued in the adventure of the Priory School for him to be a twin. But this man radiates a frightening ferality, a savagery more savage than any possessed by the most primitive of men. This could not possibly be the scion of an ancient British stock, not by any stretch of the fancy the English gentleman that Saltire had been even at the age of ten. This man had been raised in a school that made the hazing of the Priory, Rugby, and Oxford seem like the child's play that it was.

Of course, I thought, he may be mad. How otherwise account for the strange tales that floated about the clubs and the salons of our nobility and gentry?

However, I thought, he could be a product which the British occasionally turn out. Every once in a while, a son of our island, affected in some mystical way by the Orient or Africa, goes more native than the native. There was Sir Richard Francis Burton, more Arab than the Arab, and Lord John Roxton, who was said to be wilder than the Amazon Indians with whom he consorted.

During the next few minutes I decided that the first guess, that he had gone mad, was the correct one.

He said, in a deep rich baritone, "I am known as Lord Greystoke, among other things." Without offering to shake our hands or determine our identity, as any true gentleman would, he put upon the snake one naked foot, calloused an inch thick on its sole, and he pulled the arrow out. He wiped it on the grass, replaced the arrow in the quiver, and cut off the head of the reptile. While we stared in fascination and disgust, he skinned the cobra and then began biting off chunks of its meat and chewing it. The blood dripped down his chin while he stared with those beautiful but wild eyes at us.

"Would you care for some?" he said, and he grinned at us most bloodily.

"Not unless it's cooked," Holmes replied coolly.

"Cooked or raw, I'd rather starve," I said, ungrammatically but sincerely.

"Starve then," Greystoke said.

"I say," I protested. "We are fellow Englishmen, aren't we? Would you let us die of hunger while those Germans are..."

He stopped chewing, and his face became quite fierce.

"Germans!" he said. "Here? Nearby? Where are they?"

Holmes outlined our story, leaving certain parts out for security purposes. Greystoke listened him out, though impatiently, and he said, "I will kill them."

"Without giving them a chance to surrender?" I said horrifiedly.

"I don't take prisoners," he said, glaring at me. "Not any soldier, black or white, who fights for Germany. It was a band of black soldiers, under white officers, who murdered my wife and my warriors who were guarding her and burned down my house around her. I have sworn to kill every German I come across until this war ends."

He added, "And perhaps after it ends!"

"But these men are not soldiers!" I said weakly. "They are sailors, members of the Imperial German Navy!"

"They will die no less."

"Their commander dealt with us as an officer and a gentleman should," Holmes said. "In fact, we owe our lives to him."

"For that he shall have a quick and painless death."

Holmes said, "Could we at least make a fire and cook that reptile first and perhaps hear your story?"

Greystoke threw the skelton, which was stripped of most of its meat, to one side. "I'll hunt something more suitable to your civilised palates," he said. "After all, they won't get away."

He said this so grimly and assuredly that shivers ran up my spine. "And you two stay here," he said. He was gone, taken in swiftly and silently by the vegetation.

"Good God, Holmes!" I cried. "The man is a beast, a savage engine geared for vengeance! And, Holmes, whoever he is, he was certainly never the child whom we brought back safely to the duke at Pemberley House![10] Why, surely he would have recognised his saviours even though we are older! Fifteen years have not made that much difference in us!"

"But they have in him, heh?" Holmes said. "Watson, there are muddy waters in this stream. I have kept a watch on that family over the years, an infrequent watch, it is true. For some reason, we keep bumping into members of the duke's family or into people who've been involved with them. It was the duchess who shot Milverton, it was Black Peter Carey who, I strongly suspect, murdered our present Lord Greystoke's uncle, you know, the Socialist duke who drove a cab for a while..."

"In the affair of the hound of the Baskervilles?" I broke in.

"You know I don't like being interrupted, Watson," he said testily. "As I was saying, Carey probably murdered the fifth duke before he came to a bad, but deserved, end at Forest Row. I have reason to believe that Carey, under another name, was aboard the ship carrying the fifth duke's son and his wife to Africa when it was lost with all hands aboard—for all the public knew, that is. Then I was called in again by the sixth duke to find his illegimate son, who, it turned out, settled in the States instead of in Australia. It is a weird web which has tangled our fortunes with those of the Greystokes."[11]

"I just can't believe that, this man is the sixth duke's son!" I said.

"The jungle can change a man," Holmes said. "However, I agree with you, even though his features and his voice are remarkably

---

10 The true name of the ducal mansion Watson called Holdernesse Hall in "The Adventure of the Priory School." A description of the estate is found in Jane Austen's *Pride and Prejudice. Editor.*
11 For a fuller description of this involvement, see my definitive biography of Lord Greystroke. *Editor.*

similar. Our Lord Greystoke is an impostor. But how in the world did he succeed in passing himself off as the real Lord Greystoke? And when? And what happened to the sixth duke's son, the child we knew as Lord Saltire?"[12]

"Good Lord!" I said. "Do you suspect murder?"

"Anybody is capable of murder, my dear Watson," he said. "Even you and I, given the proper circumstances and the proper, or improper, state of emotion. But I have a feeling, a hunch, that this man would not be capable of cold-blooded murder. He may be emotionally unstable, though."

"Fingerprints!" I cried, elated because I had anticipated Holmes.

He smiled and said, "Yes, that would establish whether or not he is an impostor. But I doubt that there is any record of Saltire's fingerprints."

"His handwriting?" I said, somewhat crushed.

"He would search out and destroy all papers bearing Saltire's handwriting, all he could get his hands on. There must be many that he could not obtain, however, and if these could be found, we could compare Saltire's holographs with Greystoke's. I imagine that Greystoke has trained himself to write like Saltire, but an expert, myself, for instance, could easily distinguish the forgery. However, we are now in no position to do such a thing, and from the looks of things we may never be in such a position. Also, before I went to the authorities, I would make sure that the revelation would be useful. After all, we don't know why Greystoke has done this. He may be innocent of murder."

"Surely," I said, "You aren't thinking of asking Greystoke to confess?"

"What? With a high certainty that we might be killed on the spot?

---

12 It is the English custom to address the sons of noblemen with an honorary title, though legally the sons are commoners. The duke had several secondary titles, the highest of which was Marquess of Saltire. Thus, the duke's son was known as Lord Saltire. *Editor.*

And perhaps eaten? I don't think Greystoke would put us on his menu if other meat were available. If he were starving, he might not be so discriminating."

I hesitated and then I said, "I am going to confess something to you, Holmes. You remember when we were discussing Greystoke in Mycroft's office? You said that you had heard about the novel, the highly fictionalised and romanticised account of Greystoke's adventures in Africa? You also mentioned that very few copies of the novel had reached England because of the declaration of hostilities shortly before the book was published?"

"Yes?" Holmes said, looking at me strangely.

"Knowing your attitude toward my reading of what you consider trash, I did not tell you that a friend of mine in San Francisco—he was my best man when I married my first wife—sent me a copy not only of the first book but of its sequel. I have read them…"

"Good Lord!" Holmes said. "I can understand your shame, Watson, but withholding evidence…"

"What evidence?" I replied more hotly than was my wont, no doubt due to fatigue, hunger, and anxiety. "There was no crime then of which we were aware!"

"Touché!" Holmes said. "Pray accept my apologies. And continue."

"The American author, and what a wild imagination he has, pretends that the real Lord Greystoke was born in a cabin off the shore of western Africa. In his novel Greystoke's parents are marooned by mutineers. Unable to make their way back to civilisation, they build a hut and young Greystoke is born in it. When his parents die the baby is adopted by a female of a band of intelligent anthropoid apes. These apes are a product of the inflamed imagination of the author, who, by the way, has never been to Africa or apparently read much about it. To make a long story short, the boy grows up, learns to read and write

English without ever having heard a word of English…"

"Preposterous!"

"Perhaps, but the author makes it seem possible. Then a white girl, American, of course, and her family and associates, among whom is the youth who inherited the title of Greystoke…"

"Please speak in shorter sentences, Watson. And back up in your story a little."

"The girl's father had spent his life savings and borrowed heavily to purchase an old map showing where treasure was buried on an island off the African coast. His daughter went with him. They also happened to run into the true Greystoke's cousin in England, and he went along with them because he was in love with the girl."

"Quite a coincidence," said Holmes.

"And then the crew of their ship mutinied and set them down at the exact spot at which the real Greystoke's parents had been landed…"

"This Yank seems to rely heavily on coincidences," Holmes said, chuckling. "I could never understand, Watson, why you wasted your time on penny-dreadfuls."

"It's better than taking cocaine," I said.

"I fail to see why," he said. "But please get on with it."

"The real Greystoke, the jungle-born man, fell in love with the girl and rescued her a number of times."

"Naturally. And she, of course, fell in love with this inarticulate youth smelling of ape excrement…"

"It wasn't that way at all!" I cried. "Will you allow me to tell this, or should I just drop the subject?"

"My apology, Watson. I will restrain myself from making observations which are irrelevant."

"The real Greystoke's father had written a diary, in French, which the young Greystoke could not read, of course. It seemed that before the parents died, the baby had accidentally placed his ink-smeared fingers on a page of the diary. Years later, when the real Greystoke was in France, taken there by the young Frenchman who had become his friend, the diary was turned over to a fingerprint expert. Meanwhile, Greystoke followed the girl to America, only to learn that his cousin had proposed marriage and she had accepted. A short time later he received notice that his fingerprints proved that he was the real Lord Greystoke. But knowing that if the truth were revealed, his cousin would be stripped of titles and fortune, and the girl would be destitute, he nobly kept silence."

"In the finest tradition of housemaids' literature," Holmes said.

"Sneer if you like, Holmes," I said. "I thought it was very moving."

"What has all this claptrap fiction to do with our peer?"

"Why, it's as obvious as the nose on your face!"

"What's the matter with it?" Holmes said.

"It's a handsome nose," I said. "Perhaps the most famous in England since the first Duke of Wellington died. What I am saying is that the Yank must have heard something from somebody and that perhaps there is more truth in his fiction than anybody knows. He may have talked to someone who knew the true story of the Greystokes and based his novel on his inside information."

"Nonsense," Holmes said. "What happened is that the American read some newspaper or magazine accounts of how Lord Greystoke, a prime example of English eccentricity, or of madness, had abandoned his heritage, for all practical purposes, and settled down in Africa. To make matters worse, he'd gone native. No, worse than native, since no native would be caught dead living as he does, alone in the jungle, killing lions with a knife, eating meat raw, consorting with chimpanzees and gorillas. So, this Yank sees a highly sensational novel in all this and formulates a plot and characters which are bound to appeal to the public."

"Perhaps," I said. "Allow me to tell you what transpired in the sequel which the Yankee wrote."

I proceeded to do so, after which I waited for Holmes to comment. He sat leaning against a tree trunk, his brows knit, much as I have seen him sit for an entire night while he considered a case. After several minutes he burst out, "God! How I miss my pipe, Watson! Nicotine is more than an aid to thought, it is a necessity! It's a wonder that anything was done in the sciences or the arts before the discovery of America!"

Absently, he reached out and picked up a stick off the ground. He put it in his mouth, no doubt intending to suck on it as a substitute, however unsatisfactory, for the desiderated pipe. The next moment he leaped up with a yell that startled me. I cried, "What have you found, Holmes? What is it?"

"That, curse it!" he shouted and pointed at the stick. It was travelling at a fast rate on a number of thin legs toward a refuge under a log.

"Great Scott!" I said. "It's an insect, a mimetic!"

"How observant of you," he said, snarling. But the next moment he was down on his knees and groping after the creature.

"What on earth are you doing?" I said.

"It does taste like tobacco," he said. "Expediency is the mark of a…"

I never heard the rest. An uproar broke out in the jungle nearby, the shouts of men mortally wounded.

"What is it?" I said. "Could Greystoke have found the Germans?"

Then I fell silent and clutched him, as he clutched me, while a yell pierced the forest, a yell that ululated and froze our blood and hushed the wild things.

Eight

Holmes unfroze and started in the direction of the sound. I said, "Wait, Holmes! Greystoke ordered us not to leave this place! He must have his reasons for that!"

"Duke or not, he isn't going to order me around!" Holmes said. Nevertheless, he halted. It was not a change of mind about the command; it was the crashing of men thrusting through the jungle toward us. We turned and plunged into the bush in the opposite direction while a cry behind us told us that we had been seen. A moment later, heavy hands fell upon us and dragged us down. Someone gave an order in a language unknown to me, and we were jerked roughly to our feet.

Our captors were four tall men of a dark Caucasian race with features somewhat like those of the ancient Persians. They wore thick quilted helmets of some cloth, thin sleeveless shirts, short kilts, and knee-high leather boots. They were armed with small round steel shields, short heavy two-edged swords, heavy two-headed steel axes with long wooden shafts, and bows and arrows.

They said something to us. We looked blank. Then they turned as a weak cry came from the other side of the clearing. One of their own staggered out from the bush only to fall flat on his face and lie there unmoving. An arrow, which I recognised as Greystoke's, projected from his back.

Seeing this, the men became alarmed, though I suppose they had been alarmed all along. One ran out, examined the man, shook his head, and raced back. We were half-lifted, half-dragged along with them in a mad dash through vegetation that tore and ripped our clothes and us. Evidently they had run up against Greystoke, which was not a thing to be recommended at any time. I didn't know why they burdened themselves with two exhausted old men, but I surmised that it was for no beneficent purpose.

I will not recount in detail that terrible journey. Suffice it to say that we were four days and nights in the jungle, walking all day, trying to sleep at night. We were scratched, bitten, and torn, tormented with itches that wouldn't stop and sometimes sick from insect bites. We went through almost impenetrable jungle and waded waist-deep in swamps which held hordes of blood-sucking leeches. Half of the time, however, we progressed fairly swiftly along paths whose ease of access convinced me that they must be kept open by regular work parties.

The third day we started up a small mountain. The fourth day we went down it by being let down in a bamboo cage suspended by ropes from a bamboo boom. Below us lay the end of a lake that wound out of sight among the precipices that surrounded it. We were moved along at a fast pace toward a canyon into which the arm of the lake ran. Our captors pulled two dugouts out of concealment and we were paddled into the fjord. After rounding a corner, we saw before us a shore that sloped gently upward to a precipice several miles beyond it. A village of bamboo huts with thatched roofs spread along the shore and some distance inland.

The villagers came running when they saw us. A drum began beating some place, and to its beat we were marched up a narrow street and to a hut near the biggest hut. We were thrust into this, a gate of bamboo bars was lashed to the entrance, and we sat against its back wall while the villagers took turns looking in at us. As a whole, they were a good-looking people, the average of beauty being much higher than that seen in the East End of London, for instance. The women wore only long cloth skirts, though necklaces of shells hung around their necks and their long hair was decorated with flowers. The prepubescent children were stark naked.

Presently, food was brought to us. This consisted of delicious baked fish, roasted pygmy antelope, unleavened bread, and a brew that would under other circumstances have been too sweet for my taste. I am not ashamed to admit that Holmes and I gorged ourselves, devouring everything set before us.

I went to sleep shortly afterward, waking after dusk with a start. A torch flared in a stanchion just outside the entrance, at which two guards stood. Holmes was sitting near it, reading his *Practical Handbook of Bee Culture, With Some Observations Upon the Segregation of the Queen.* "Holmes," I began, but he held up his hand for silence. His keen ears had detected a sound a few seconds before mine did. This swelled to a hubbub with the villagers swarming out while the drum beat again. A moment later we saw the cause of the uproar. Six warriors, with Reich and Von Bork among them, were marching toward us. And while we watched curiously the two Germans were shoved into our hut.

Though both were much younger than Holmes and I, they were in equally bad condition—probably, I suppose, because they had not practiced the good old British custom of walking whenever possible. Von Bork refused to talk to us, but Reich, always a gentleman, told us what had happened to his party.

"We too heard the noises and that horrible cry," he said. "We made our way cautiously toward it, until we saw the carnage in a clearing. There were five dead men sprawled there, and six running in one direction and four in another. Standing with his foot on the chest of the largest corpse was a white man clad only in a leopard-skin. He was the one uttering that awful cry, which I would swear no human throat could make."

"*Der englisch Affenmensch,*" Von Bork muttered, his only contribution to the conversation that evening.

"Three of the men had arrows in them; the other two obviously had had their necks broken," Reich continued. "Von Bork whispered to me the wild man's identity, and so I whispered to my men to fire at him. Before we could do so, he had leaped up and pulled himself by a branch into a tree, and he was gone. We searched for him for some time without success. Then we started out to the east, but at dusk one of my men fell with an arrow through his neck. The angle of the arrow showed that it had come from above. We looked upward but could see nothing. Then a voice, speaking in excellent German, with a Branden-burger accent yet, ordered us to turn back. We were to march to the southwest. If we did not, one of us would die at dusk each day until no one was left. I asked him why we should do this, but there was no reply. Obviously, he had us entirely at his mercy—which, I suspected, from the looks of him, he utterly lacked."

"He claims that German officers murdered his wife," Holmes said.

"That's a lie!" Reich said indignantly. "More British propaganda! We are not the baby-bayoneting Huns your propaganda office portrays us as being!"

"There are some bad apples in every barrel," Holmes replied coolly.

Reich looked as if something had suddenly disturbed him. I thought it was a gas pain, but he said, "So, then, you *met* Greystoke! *He* told you this! But why did he desert you, leave you to fall into the hands of these savages?"

"I don't know," Holmes said. "Please carry on with your story."

"My first concern was the safety and well-being of my men. To have ignored Greystoke would have been to be brave but stupid. So I ordered the march to the southwest. After two days if became evident that Greystoke intended for us to starve to death. All our food was stolen that night, and we dared not leave the line of march to hunt, even though I doubt that we would have been able to shoot anything. The evening of the second day, I called out, begging that he let us at least hunt for food. He must have had some pangs of conscience, some mercy in him after all. That morning we woke to find a freshly killed wild pig, one of those orange-bristled swine, in the center of the camp. From somewhere in the branches overhead his voice came mockingly. 'Pigs should eat pigs!'

"And so we struggled southwestward until today. We were attacked by these people. Greystoke had not ordered us to lay down our arms, so we gave a good account of ourselves. But only Von Bork and I survived, and we were knocked unconscious by the flats of their axes. And marched here, the Lord only knows for what end."

"I suspect that the Lord of the Jungle, one of Greystoke's unofficial titles, knows," Holmes said glumly.

Nine

If Greystoke did know, he did not appear to tell us what to expect. Several days passed while we slept and ate and talked to Reich. Von Bork continued to ignore us, even though Holmes several times addressed him. Holmes asked him about his health, which I thought a strange concern for a man who had not killed us only because he lacked the opportunity.

Holmes seemed especially interested in his left eye, once coming up to within a few inches of it and staring at it. Von Bork became enraged at this close scrutiny.

"Get away from me, British swine!" he yelled. "Or I will ruin both of your eyes!"

"Permit Dr. Watson to examine it," Holmes said. "He might be able to save it."

"I want no incompetent English physician poking around it," Von Bork said.

I became so indignant that I lectured him on the very high standards of British medicine, but he only turned his back on me.

Holmes chuckled at this and winked at me.

At the end of the week, we were allowed to leave the hut during the day, unaccompanied by guards. Holmes and I were not restrained in any way, though the Germans were hobbled with shackles so that they could not walk very fast. Apparently, our captors decided that Holmes and I were too old to give them much of a run for their money.

We took advantage of our comparative freedom to stroll around the village, inspecting everything and also attempting to learn the language.

"I don't know what family it belongs to," Holmes said. "But it is related neither to Cornish nor Chaldean, of that I'm sure."

Holmes was also interested in the white china of these people, which represented their highest art form. The black figures and designs they painted upon it reminded me somewhat of early Greek vase paintings. The vases and dishes were formed from kaolin deposits which existed to the north near the precipices. I mention this only because the white clay was to play an important part in our salvation in the near future.

At the end of the second week, Holmes, a superb linguist, had attained some fluency in the speech of our captors. "It belongs to a completely unknown language family," he said. "But there are certain words which, degenerated though they are, obviously come from ancient Persian. I would say that at one time these people had contact with a wandering party of descendants of Darius. The party settled down here, and these people borrowed some words from their idiom."

The village consisted of a hundred huts arranged in concentric circles. Each held a family ranging from two to eight members. Their fields lay north of the village on the slopes leading up to the precipices. The stock consisted of goats, pigs, and dwarf antelopes.

Their alcoholic drink was a sort of mead made from the honey of wild bees. A few specimens of these ventured near the village, and Holmes secured some for study. They were about an inch long, striped black and white, and were armed with a long venom-ejecting barb. Holmes declared that they were of a new species, and he saw no reason not to classify them as *Apis holmesi*.

Once a week a party set out to the hills to collect honey. Its members were always clad in leather clothing and gloves and wore veils over their hats. Holmes asked permission to accompany them, explaining that he was wise in the ways of bees. To his disappointment, they refused him. A further inquiry by him resulted in the information that there was a negotiable, though difficult, pass through the precipices. It was used only for emergency purposes because of the vast number of bees that filled the narrow pass. Holmes obtained his data by questioning a child. Apparently, the adults had not thought to tell their young to keep silent about this means of exit.

"The bee-warding equipment is kept locked up in their temple," Holmes said. "And that makes it impossible to obtain it for an escape attempt."

The temple was the great hut in the village's centre. We were not allowed to enter it or even to approach it within fifty feet. Through some discreet inquiries, and unashamed eavesdropping, Holmes discovered that the high priestess-and-queen lived within the temple. We had never seen her nor were we likely to do so. She had been born in the temple and was to reside there until she died. Just why she was so restricted Holmes could not determine. His theory was that she was a sort of hostage to the gods.

"Perhaps, Watson, she is confined because of a superstition that arose after the catastrophe which their myths say deluged this land and the great civilisation it harboured. The fishermen tell me that they often see on the bottom of this lake the sunken ruins of the stone houses in which their ancestors lived. A curse was laid upon the land, they say, and they hint that only by keeping the high priestess-cum-queen inviolate, unseen by profane eyes, untouched by anyone after pubescence, can the wrath of the gods be averted. They are cagey in what they say, so I have had to surmise certain aspects of their religion."

"That's terrible!" I said.

"The deluge?"

"No, that a woman should be denied freedom and love."

"She has a name, but I have never overheard it. They refer to her as The Beautiful One."

"Is there nothing we can do for her?" I said.

"I do not know that she wants to be helped. You must not allow your well-known gallantry to endanger us. But to satisfy a legitimate scientific interest, if anthropology is a science, we could perhaps attempt a look inside the temple. Its roof has a large circular hole in its center. If we could get near the top of the high tree about twenty yards from it, we could look down into the building."

"With the whole village watching us?" I said. "No, Holmes, it is impossible to get up the tree unobserved during the day. And if we did so during the night, we could see nothing because of the darkness. In any event, it would probably mean instantaneous death even to make the attempt."

"There are torches lit in the building at night," he said. "Come, Watson, if you have no taste for this arboreal adventure, I shall go it alone."

And that was why, despite my deep misgivings, we climbed that towering tree on a cloudy night. After Von Bork and Reich had fallen asleep and our guards, had dozed off and the village was silent except for a chanting in the temple, we crept out of our hut. Holmes had hidden a rope the day before, but even with this it was no easy task. We were not youths of twenty, agile as monkeys and as fearless aloft. Holmes threw the weighted end of the rope over the lowest branch, which was twenty feet up, and tied the two ends together.

Then, grasping the rope with both hands, and bracing his feet against the trunk, he half-walked, almost perpendicular to the trunk, up the tree. On reaching the branch, he rested for a long time while he gasped for breath so loudly that I feared he would wake up the nearest villagers. When he was quite recovered, he called down to me to make the ascent. Since I was heavier and several years older, and lacked his feline muscles, having more the physique of a bear, I experienced great difficulty in getting up. I wrapped my legs around the rope—no walking at a ninety-degree angle to the tree for me—and painfully and gaspingly hauled myself up. But I persisted—after all, I am British—and Holmes pulled me up at the final stage of what I was beginning to fear was my final journey.

After resting, we made a somewhat easier ascent via the branches to a position about ten feet below the top of the tree. From there we could look almost directly down through the hole in the middle of the roof. The torches within enabled us to see its interior quite clearly.

Both of us gasped when we saw the woman standing in the centre of the building by a stone altar. She was a beautiful woman, surely one of the daintiest things that ever graced this planet. She had long golden hair and eyes that looked dark from where we sat but which, we later found out, were a deep grey. She was wearing nothing except a necklace of some stones that sparkled as she moved. Though I was fascinated, I also felt something of shame, as if I were a peeping tom. I had to remind myself that the women wore nothing above the waist in their everyday attire and that when they swam in the lake they wore nothing at all. So we were doing nothing immoral by this spying.

Despite this reasoning, my face (and other things) felt inflamed.[13]

She stood there, doing nothing for a long time, which I expected would make Holmes impatient. He did not stir or make any comment, so I suppose that this time he did not mind a lack of action. The priestesses chanted and the priests walked around in a circle making signs with their hands and their fingers. Then a bound he-goat was brought in and placed on the altar, and, after some more mumbo-jumbo, the woman cut its throat. The blood was caught in a golden bowl and passed around in a sort of communion, the woman drinking first.

"A most unsanitary arrangement," I murmured to Holmes.

"These people are, nevertheless, somewhat cleaner than your average Londoner," Holmes replied. "And much more cleanly than your Scots peasant."

I was about to take umbrage at this, since I am of Scots descent on my mother's side. Holmes knew both this and my sensitivity about it. He had been making too many remarks of this nature recently, and though I attributed them to irritability arising from nicotine withdrawal, I was, to use an American phrase, getting fed up with them. I was about to remonstrate when my heart leaped into my throat and choked me.

A hand had come from above and clamped down upon my shoulder. I knew that it wasn't Holmes' because I could see both of his hands.

---

13 The parentheses are the editor's. Watson had crossed out this phrase, though not enough to make it illegible. *Editor.*

Ten

Holmes almost fell off the branch but was saved by another hand, which grasped him by the collar of his shirt. A familiar voice said, "Silence!"

"Greystoke!" I gasped. And then, remembering that, after all, he was a duke, I said, "Your pardon. I mean, Your Grace."

"What are you doing up here, you baboon!" Holmes said.

I was shocked at this, though I knew that Holmes spoke thus only because he must have been thoroughly frightened. To address a high British nobleman in this manner was not his custom.

"Tut, tut, Holmes," I said.

"Tut, tut yourself," he replied. "He's not paying me a fee! He's no client of mine. Besides, I doubt that he is entitled to his title!"

A growl that lifted the hairs on the back of my neck came from above. It was followed by the descent of the duke's heavy body upon our branch, which bent alarmingly. But Greystoke squatted upon it, his hands free, with all the ease of the baboon he had been accused of being.

"What does that last remark mean?" he said.

At that moment the moon broke through the clouds. A ray fell upon Holmes' face, which was as pale as when he had been playing the dying detective. He said, "This is neither the time nor the place for an investigation of your credentials. We are in a desperate plight, and…"

"You don't realise how desperate," Greystoke said. "I usually abide by human laws when I am in civilisation or among the black blood-brothers of my ranch in East Africa. But when I am in my larger estate, that of Central Africa, when I am in the jungle, where I have a higher rank even than duke, where, to put it simply, I am the king, where I revert to my primal and happiest state, that of a great ape…"

Good Lord! I thought. And this is the man Holmes referred to as inarticulate!

"…then I obey only my own laws, not those of humanity, for which I have the greatest contempt, barring a few specimens of such…"

There was much more in this single statement, the length of which would have made any German philosopher proud. The gist of it was that if Holmes did not explain his remark now, he would have no chance to do so later. Nor was the duke backward in stating that I would not be taking any news of Holmes' fate to the outside world.

"He means it, Holmes!" I said.

"I am well aware of that, Watson," he answered. "His Grace is covered only with a thin veneer of civilisation."

This phrase, I remembered, was one used often by the American novelist to describe his protagonist's assumption of human culture.

"Very well, Your Highness," Holmes said. "It is not my custom to set forth a theory until I have enough evidence to make it a fact. But under the circumstances…"

I looked for Greystoke to show some resentment at Holmes' sarcastic use of a title appropriate only to a monarch. He, however, only smiled. This, I believe, was a reaction of pleasure, of ignorance of

Holmes' intent to cut him. He was sure that he deserved the title, and now that I have had time to reflect on it, I agree with him. Though a duke in England, in Africa he ruled a kingdom many times larger than our tight little isle. And he paid no taxes in it.

"Watson and I were acquainted with the ten-year-old son of the sixth duke, your reputed father," Holmes said. "That boy, the then Lord Saltire, is *not* you. Yet you have the title that should be his. You notice that I do not say the title should *rightly* be his. You are the legitimate inheritor of the late duke's titles and estates. Titles and estates, by the way, that should never have been his or his son's."

"Good Lord, Holmes!" I said. "What are you saying?"

"If you will refrain from interrupting, you will hear what I'm saying," he responded sharply. "Your Grace, that American novelist who has written a highly fictionalised novel based on your rather... ahem... nonconventional behaviour in Africa, came closer to the truth than anybody but yourself, and a few of your friends, I presume, realise. Watson tells me that in the novel your father, who should have been the seventh duke, was marooned on the shores of western Africa with his wife. There you were born, and when your parents died, you were adopted by a tribe of large intelligent apes hitherto unknown to science. They were strictly a product of a romantic imagination, of course, and the apes must have been either chimpanzees or gorillas, both of which du Chaillu has reported seeing in West Africa. Neither, however, exists at ten degrees south latitude, which is where the novelist said you were born and raised. I would place your birth further north, say somewhere near or in the very country, Gabon, which du Chaillu visited."

"Elementary, my dear Holmes," Greystoke said, smiling slightly again. I warmed to him somewhat, since it was evident by his remark that he was acquainted with my narratives of the adventures of Holmes and myself. A man who read these, and with evident pleasure, couldn't be all bad.

"If it is elementary," Holmes said with some asperity, "I am still the only man complex enough to have grasped the truth."

"Not all of it," Greystoke replied. "That Yank writer was quite correct in his guess that the tribe that raised me was unknown to science. However, they were not great apes but a sort of apemen, beings halfway on the evolutionary ladder between *Homo sapiens* and the ape. They had speech, which, though simple, was still speech. And that is why I did not become incapable of using language, as all other feral humans so far discovered have been incapable. Once a child passes a certain age without encountering human speech, he is mentally retarded."

"Really?" Holmes said.

"It does not matter whether or not you believe that," the duke said.

"But the Yank had your uncle inheriting the title after his brother died and your parents were declared dead. Then your uncle, the sixth duke, died, and your cousin, the lad Watson and I knew as Lord Saltire, became the seventh duke. So far, the Yank's account was in agreement with the reality. It is the next event which, in his romance, departed completely from reality."

"And that was?" Greystoke said softly.

"Consider first what the Yank said happened. In his novel the jungle man found out that he was the rightful heir to the title. But he kept silent about it because he loved the heroine and she had promised to marry his cousin and considered herself bound by her promise. If he revealed the truth, he would strip her of her title of duchess and, worse, of the fortune which the cousin possessed. She would be penniless again. So he nobly said nothing.

"But according to Watson, a great reader of fiction, the Yank wrote a sequel to the first romance. In this the cousin gets sick and before dying confesses that he saw the telegram about the fingerprints, destroyed it, and ignobly kept silent. Fortunately, the girl had put off the marriage, so there is no question of her being a virgin, which is an important issue to the housemaids and some doctors who read this type of literature. Our hero becomes Lord Greystoke and everybody lives happily forever after—until the next adventure.

"I believe that in reality you did marry the girl on whom the novelist based his character. But that is pure nonsense about the jungle man's assumption of the title. If that had happened in reality, do you think for a moment that the resultant publicity would not have been world-wide? What a story—the heir to an English title appearing out of the African forest, an heir not even known to exist, an heir who has been raised by a band of missing links. Can you imagine the commotion, the curiosity, inflaming the world? Can you imagine what a hell the heir's life would be, no privacy, reporters trailing him at every step, an utter lack of privacy for not only him but his wife and his family?

"But we know that no such thing happened. We do know that an English peer who had led an uneventful life, except for being kidnapped when ten, at maturity goes to Africa and settles down upon a ranch. And after a while strange tales seep back to London, tales of this peer reverting to a jungle life, wandering through central Africa clad only in a loincloth, eating raw meat, killing lions with only a knife, breaking the necks of gorillas with full-nelsons, and consorting with apes and elephants. The man has suddenly become a combination of Hercules, Ulysses, and Mowgli. And Croesus, I might add, since he seems to have a source of great wealth hidden some place in deepest Africa. It is distributed through illegal channels, but word of it reaches Threadneedle Street and New Scotland Yard, of course.

"I wonder," he added after a pause, "if this valley could be where the gold comes from?"

"No," Greystoke, said. "That is a long way off. This valley is mostly lake, rich only with fish life. Once it was a wealthy, even grand, land with a civilisation to rival Egypt's. But it was flooded when a natural dam caved in after an earthquake, and all its works and most of its people were drowned. When the water is clear you can see at noon the roof-tops and toppled pillars here and there. Today, the degenerate descendants of the survivors huddle in this miserable village and talk of the great days, of the glory of Zu-Vendis."

"Zu-Vendis!" I exclaimed. "But..."

The duke made an impatient sound and said, "Carry on, Holmes."

"First, allow me to ask you a question. Did that Yank somehow hear an account of your life that was not available to the public? A distorted account, perhaps, but still largely valid?"

Greystoke nodded and said, "A friend of mine with a drinking problem, while on a binge, told a fellow some things which seem to have been relayed to the Yank. The Yank included parts of this account in his novel."

"I surmised such. He thought he had the true story of your life, but he didn't dare present it as anything but fiction. For one thing, he could be sued. For another, your passion for vengeance is rather well known.

"In any event, his story of how you came into your title, though fictional, still contains the clue needed to determine, the true story.

"Here, as I reconstruct it, is what happened. You knew that you were the true heir. You wanted the title and the girl and everything, though I suspect that without the girl you would not have cared for the other."

Greystoke nodded.

"Very well. Your cousin's yacht had been temporarily put out of commission, not wrecked and sunk, as was depicted in the novel. You had met the party from the yacht; they were stranded on the shore near your natal cabin. All that nonsense in the second novel about your girl being abducted by little hairy men from the hidden city of treasure deep in the heart of Africa was just that, nonsense."

"If it had been true," Greystoke said, "the abductors would have been forced to travel a thousand miles through the worst part of Africa, abduct my wife, and travel back to their ruins. And then, when I rescued her, she and I would have had to travel another thousand miles back to the yacht. Under the circumstances, this would have taken several years, and the time for that allowed in the novel just did not suffice. Besides, it was all imagination. Except for the city itself and the degenerates who inhabit it."

"That high priestess who fell in love with you...?" I said.

"Carry on, Holmes," he said.

"After your cousin died, your girl and your friends told you what a lack of privacy you and your family would have from then on. So you all decided to carry out a fraud. Yet, it was not really a fraud, since you were the legitimate heir. You looked much like your cousin, and so you decided to pass yourself off as him. When the yacht returned to England, for all anyone knew, it had made a routine voyage from England and around Africa and back again. Your friends coached you in all you needed to know about the friends and acquaintances you would meet. The servants at your ancestral estate may have detected something a little strange about you, but you probably had an excuse trumped up. A temporary fit of amnesia, perhaps."

"Correct," Greystoke said. "I used that excuse often. I was always running into somebody about whom I'd not been instructed. And occasionally I'd do something very un-British."[14]

"Lord, the mystery of the century!" cried Holmes. "And I can't say a word about it!"

"How do I know I can trust you?" Greystoke said.

---

[14] This disclosure definitely invalidates some of my speculations and reconstructions in my biography of Greystoke. These will be corrected in a future issue. Lord Greystoke himself had admitted that Holmes' theory is correct. See "Extracts from the Memoirs of Lord Greystoke," *Mother Was A Lovely Beast*, Philip José Farmer, editor, Chilton, October 1974.

At these words my mounting anxiety reached its peak. I had wondered why Greystoke was so frank, and then the sickening certainty came that he did not care what we had learned because dead men cannot talk. The only hope I had was that Greystoke had not murdered his cousin after all. Perhaps he was a decent fellow under all that savagery. This hope collapsed when I considered the possibility that he might not have been altogether frank. What if he had murdered his cousin?

Though I felt that it was dangerous to pursue this subject, I could not restrain my curiosity. "Your Grace," I said, "I hope that you won't think I'm too inquisitive. But... just what did happen to your cousin? Did he die as described in the second novel, die of a jungle fever after making a deathbed confession that he had cheated you out of your birthright and your lover? Or...?"

"Or did I slit his throat?" Greystoke said. "No, Dr. Watson, I did not kill him, though I must admit that the thought of doing so did cross my mind. And I was glad that he died, but, unlike so many of you civilised creatures, I felt no guilt about being glad. Nor would I feel any regret, shame, or guilt in putting anyone out of the way who was a grave threat to me or mine. Does that answer your question?"

"More than sufficiently, Your Grace," I said, gulping. He may have been lying, but my hopes rose again when I reflected that he did not have to lie if he intended to kill us.

"You have implied that you have read Watson's narratives," Holmes said. "Admittedly, they are somewhat exaggerated and romanticised. But his portrayal of our moral character is quite accurate. Our word is our bond."

Greystoke said, "Hmmm!" and he frowned. He fondled the hilt of the huge knife in his scabbard, and I felt as cold as the moon looked. As dead, too.

Holmes seemed to be more meditative than frightened. He said, slowly, "We are professional men, Your Grace. If we were to take you as our client, we could not disclose a word of the case. Not even the police could force it from us."

"Ah!" Greystoke said, smiling grimly. "I am always forgetting the immense value civilised people put upon money. Of course! I pay you a fee and your lips are shut forever."

"Or until such time as Your Grace releases us from the sacred bonds of confidentiality."

"What would you consider a reasonable fee?"

"The highest I ever earned was in the case of the Priory School," said Holmes. "It was your uncle who paid it. Twelve thousand pounds."

He repeated, savouring the words, "Twelve thousand pounds."

Quickly, he added, "Of course, that sum was my fee. Watson, as my partner, received the same amount."

"Really, Holmes," I murmured.

"Twenty-four thousand pounds," the duke said, still frowning.

"That was in 1901," Holmes said. "Inflation has sent prices sky-high since then, and the income tax rate is ascending as if it were a rocket."

"For Heaven's sake, Holmes!" I cried. "I do not see the necessity for this fishmarket bargaining! Surely…"

Holmes coldly interrupted. "You will please leave the financial arrangements to me, the senior partner and the true professional in this matter."

"You'll antagonise His Grace, and…"

"Would sixty thousand pounds be adequate?" Greystoke said.

"Well," Holmes said, hesitating, "God knows how wartime conditions will continue to cheapen the price of money in the next few years."

Suddenly, the knife was in the duke's hands. He made no threatening moves with it. He merely looked at it as if he were considering cleaning it.

"Your Grace is most generous," Holmes said quickly. Greystoke put the knife back into the scabbard.

"I don't happen to have a cheque on me," he said. "You will trust me until we get to Nairobi?"

"Certainly, Your Grace," Holmes murmured. "Your family was always the most open-handed in my experience. Now, the king of Holland…"

"What is this you said about Zu-Vendis?" I broke in, knowing that Holmes would take a long time to describe a case some of whose aspects still rankled him.

"Who cares?" Holmes said, but I ignored him. "As I remember it, an Englishman, a great hunter and explorer, wrote a book describing his adventures in that country. His name was Allan Quatermain."

Greystoke nodded and said, "I've read some of his biographical accounts."

"I thought they were novels," Holmes said. "Must we discuss cheap fiction…" His voice trailed as he realised that Greystoke had said that Zu-Vendis was a reality.

Greystoke said, "Either Quatermain or his agent and editor, H. R. Haggard, exaggerated the size of Zu-Vendis. It was supposed to be about the size of France but actually covered an area equal to that of Liechtenstein. In the main, however, except for the size and location of Zu-Vendis, Quatermain's account is true. He was accompanied on his expedition by two Englishmen, a baronet, Sir Henry Curtis, and a naval captain, John Good. And that great Zulu warrior, Umslopogaas, a man whom I would have liked to have known. After the Zulu and Quatermain died, Curtis sent Quatermain's manuscript of the adventure to Haggard. Haggard apparently added some things of his own to give more verisimilitude to the chronicle. For one thing, he said that several British commissions were investigating Zu-Vendis with the intent of finding a more accessible means of travel to it. This was not so. Zu-Vendis was never found, and that is why most people concluded that the account was pure fiction. Shortly after the manuscript was sent out by one of the natives who had accompanied the Quatermain party, the entire valley except for this high end was flooded."

"Then poor Curtis and Good and their lovely Zu-Vendis wives were drowned?" I said.

"No," Greystoke said. "They were among the dozen or so who reached safety. Apparently, they either could not get out of the valley then or decided to stay here. After all, Nylepthah, Curtis' wife, was the queen, and she would not want to abandon her people, few though they were. The two Englishmen settled down, taught the people the use of the bow, among other things, and died here. They were buried up in the hills."

"What a sad story!" I said.

"All people must die," Greystoke replied, as if that told the whole story of the world. And perhaps it did.

Greystoke looked out at the temple, saying, "That woman at whom you two have been staring with a not-quite-scientific detachment..."

"Yes?" I said.

"Her name is also Nylepthah. She is the granddaughter of both Good and Curtis."

Eleven

Great Scott!" I said. "A British woman parading around naked before those savages!"

Greystoke shrugged and said, "It's their custom."

"We must rescue her and get her back to the home of her ancestors!" I cried.

"Be quiet, Watson, or you'll have the whole pack howling for our blood," Holmes growled. "She seems quite contented with her lot. Or could it be," he added, looking hard at me, "that you have once again fallen into love?"

He made it sound as if the grand passion were an open privy. Blushing, I said, "I must admit that there is a certain feeling..."

"Well, the fair sex is your department," he said. "But really, Watson, at your age!"

("The Americans have a proverb," I said. "The older the buck, the stiffer the horn.")[15]

---

15 The parentheses are the editor's, indicating another passage crossed out by Watson.

"Be quiet, both of you," the duke said. "I permitted the Zu-Vendis to capture you because I knew you'd be safe for a while. I had to get on up-country to check out a rumour that a white woman was being held captive by a tribe of blacks. Though I am positive that my wife is dead, still there is always hope. Mr. Holmes suggested that the Germans might have played a trick on me by substituting the charred body of a native girl. That had occurred to me previously. That I wear only a loincloth doesn't mean that I am naked of intelligence.[16]

"I found the white girl, an Englishwoman, but she was not my wife…"

"Good heavens!" I said. "Where is she? Have you hidden her out there?"

"She's still with the sultan of the tribe," he said sourly. "I went to much trouble to rescue her, had to kill a dozen or so tribesmen getting to her, and a dozen on the way out. And then the woman told me she was perfectly happy with the sultan and would I please return her. I told her to find her own way back. I detest violence which can be avoided. If only she had told me beforehand…. Well, that's all over."

I did not comment. I thought it indiscreet to point out that the woman could not have told him how she felt until *after* he had fought his way in. And I doubted that she had an opportunity to voice her opposition on the way out.

"I drove the Germans this way because I expected that they would, like you, be picked up by the Zu-Vendis. Tomorrow night, all four of you prisoners are scheduled to be sacrificed on the temple altar. I got back an hour ago to get you two out."

"That was cutting it close, wasn't it?" Holmes said.

"You mean to leave Von Bork and Reich here?" I said. "To be

---

16 Apparently, Watson forgot to describe Holmes' comment. Undoubtedly, he would have inserted it at the proper place in the final draft.

slaughtered like sheep? And what about the woman, Nylepthah? What kind of life is that, being confined from birth to death in that house, being denied the love and companionship of a husband, forced to murder poor devils of captives?"

"Yes," said Holmes. "Reich is a very decent fellow and should be treated like a prisoner of war. I wouldn't mind at all if Von Bork were to die, but only he knows the location of the SB papers. The fate of Britain, of her allies, hangs on those papers. As for the woman, well, she is of good British stock and it seems a shame to leave her here in this squalidness."

"So she can go to London and perhaps live in squalour there?" Greystoke said.

"I'll see to it that that does not happen," I said. "Your Grace, you can have back my fee if you take that woman along."

Greystoke laughed softly and said, "I couldn't refuse a man who loves love more than he loves money. And you can keep the fee."

Twelve

A t some time before dawn, Greystoke entered our hut. The Germans were also waiting for him, since we had told them what to expect if they did not leave with us. The duke gestured for silence, unnecessarily, I thought, and we followed him outside. The two guards, gagged and trussed-up, lay by the door. Near them stood Nylepthah, also gagged, her hands bound before her and a rope hobbling her. Her glorious body was concealed in a cloak. The duke removed the hobble, gestured at us, took the woman by the arm, and we walked silently through the village. Our immediate goal was the beach, where we intended to steal two boats. We would paddle to the foot of the cliff on top of which was the bamboo boom and ascend the ropes. Then we would cut the ropes so that we could not be followed. Greystoke had come down on the rope after disposing of the guards at the boom. He would climb back up the rope and then pull us up.

Our plans died in the bud. As we approached the beach, we saw torches flaring on the water. Presently, as we watched from behind a hut, we saw fishermen paddling in with their catch of night-caught fish.

Someone stirred in the hut beside which we crouched, and before we could get away, a woman, yawning and stretching came out. She must have been waiting for her fisherman husband. Whatever the case, she surprised us.

The duke moved swiftly, but too late, toward her. She screamed loudly, and though she quit almost immediately, she had aroused the village.

There is no need to go into detail about the long and exhausting run we made through the village, while the people poured out, and up the slopes toward the faraway pass in the precipices. Greystoke smote right and left and before him, and men and women went down like the Philistines before Samson. We were armed with the short swords he had stolen from the armory and so were of some aid to him. But by the time we had left the village and reached the fields, Holmes and I were breathing very hard.

"You two help the woman along between you," the duke commanded the Germans. Before we could protest, though what good it would have done if we had I don't know, we were picked up, one under each arm, and carried off. Burdened though he was, Greystoke ran faster than the three behind him. The ground, only about a foot away from my face since I was dangling like a rag doll in his arm, reeled by. After about a mile, the duke stopped and released us. He did this by simply dropping us. My face hit the dirt at the same time my knees did. I was somewhat pained, but I thought it indiscreet to complain. Holmes, however, displayed a knowledge of swear words which would have delighted a dock worker. Greystoke ignored him, urging us to push on. Far behind us we could see the torches of our pursuers and hear their clamour.

By dawn the Zu-Vendis had gotten closer. All of us, except for the indefatigable duke, were tiring swiftly. The pass was only half a mile away, and once we were through that, the duke said, we would be safe. The savages behind us, though, were beginning to shoot their arrows at us.

"We can't get through the pass anyway!" I said between gasps to Holmes. "We have no equipment to keep the bees off us! If the arrows don't kill us, the bee-stings will!"

Ahead of us, where the hills suddenly moved in and formed the entrance to the path, a vast buzzing filled the air. Fifty thousand tiny, but deadly, insects swirled in a thick cloud as they prepared to voyage to the sea of flowers which held the precious nectar.

We stopped to catch our breath and consider the situation.

"We can't go back and we can't go ahead!" I said. "What shall we do?"

"I still live!" the duke cried. This, I thought, was an admirable motto, but it was of no help at all to us. Greystoke, however, was a practical man. He pointed at the nearby hill, at the base of which was the white clay used by the Zu-Vendis to make their fine pots and dishes.

"Coat yourselves with that!" he said. "It should be somewhat of a shield!" And he hastened to take his own advice.

I hesitated. The duke had stripped off his loincloth and had jumped into the stream which ran nearby. Then he had scooped out with his hands a quantity of clay, had mixed it with water, and was smearing it over him everywhere. Holmes was removing his clothing before going into the stream. The Germans were getting ready to do likewise, while the beautiful Nylepthah stood abandoned. I did the only thing a gentleman could do. I went to her and removed her cloak, under which she wore nothing. I told her in my halting Zu-Vendis that I was ready to sacrifice myself for her. Though the bees, alarmed, were now moving in a great cloud toward us, I would make sure that I smeared the clay all over her before I took care of myself.

Nylepthah said, "I know an easier way to escape the bees. Let me run back to the village."

"Poor deluded girl!" I said. "You do not know what is best for you! Trust me, and I will see you safely to England, the home of your ancestors. And then…"

I did not get a chance to promise to marry her. Holmes and the Germans cried out, causing me to look up just in time to see Greystoke falling unconscious to the ground. An arrow had hit him in the head, and though it had struck a glancing blow, it had knocked him out and made a large nasty wound.

I thought we were indeed lost. Behind us was the howling horde of savages, their arrows and spears and axes flying through the air at us. Ahead was a swarm of giant bees, a cloud so dense that I could barely see the hills behind them. The buzzing was deafening. The one man who was strong enough and jungle-wise enough to pull us through was out of action for the time being. And if the bees attacked soon, which they would do, he would be in that state permanently. So would all of us.

Holmes shouted at me, "Never mind taking advantage of that woman, Watson! Come here, quickly, and help me!"

"This is no time to indulge in jealousy, Holmes," I muttered, but nevertheless I obeyed him. "No, Watson," Holmes said, "I'll put on the clay! You daub on me that excellent black dirt there along the banks of the stream! Put it on in stripes, thus, white and black alternating!"

"Have you gone mad, Holmes?" I said.

"There's no time to talk," said Holmes. "The bees are almost upon us! Oh, they are deadly, deadly, Watson! Quick, the mud!"

Within a minute, striped like a zebra, Holmes stood before me. He ran to the pile of clothes and took from the pocket of his jacket the large magnifying glass that had been his faithful companion all these years.

And then he did something that caused me to cry out in utter despair. He ran directly toward the deadly buzzing cloud.

I shouted after him as I ran to drag him away from his futile and senseless act. It was too late to get him away from the swiftly advancing insects. I knew that, just as I knew that I would die horribly with him. Nevertheless, I would be with him. We had been comrades too many years for me to even contemplate for a second abandoning him.

He turned when he heard my voice and shouted, "Go back, Watson! Go back! Get the others to one side! Drag Greystoke out of their path! I know what I'm doing! Get away! I command you, Watson!"

The conditioning of our many years of association turned me and sent me back to the group. I'd obeyed his orders too long to refuse them now. But I was weeping, convinced that he was out of his mind, or, if he did have a plan, it would fail. I got Reich to help me drag the senseless and heavily bleeding Greystoke half into the stream, and I ordered Von Bork and Nylepthah to lie down in the stream. The clay coating, I was convinced, was not an adequate protection. We could submerge ourselves when the bees passed over us. The stream was only inches deep, but perhaps the water flowing over our bodies would discourage the insects.

Lying in the stream, holding Greystoke's head up to keep him from drowning, I watched Holmes.

He had indeed gone crazy. He was dancing around and around, stopping now and then to bend over and wiggle his buttocks in a most undignified manner. Then he would hold up the magnifying glass so that the sunlight flashed through it at the Zu-Vendis. These, by the way, had halted to stare open-mouthed at Holmes.

"Whatever are you doing?" I shouted.

He shook his head angrily at me to indicate that I should keep quiet. At that moment I became aware that he was himself making a loud buzzing sound. It was almost submerged in the louder noise of the swarm, but I was near enough to hear it faintly.

Again and again Holmes whirled, danced, stopped, pointing his wriggling buttocks at the Zu-Vendis savages and letting the sun pass through the magnifying glass at a certain angle. His actions seemed to puzzle not only the humans but the bees. The swarm had stopped its forward movement and it was hanging in the air, seemingly pointed at Holmes.

Suddenly, as Holmes completed his obscene dance for the seventh time, the swarm flew forward. I cried out, expecting to see him covered with the huge black-and-white-striped horrors. But the mass split in two, leaving him an island in their midst. And then they were all gone, and the Zu-Vendis were running away screaming, their bodies black and fuzzy with a covering of bees. Some of them dropped in their flight, rolling back and forth, screaming, batting at the insects, and then becoming still and silent.

I ran to Holmes, crying, "How did you do it?"

"Do you remember your scepticism when I told you that I had made an astounding discovery? One that will enshrine my name among the greats in the hall of science?"

"You don't mean…?"

He nodded. "Yes, bees do have a language, even African bees. It is actually a system of signals, not a true language. Bees who have discovered a new source of honey return to the hive and there perform a dance which indicates clearly the direction of and the distance at which the honey lies. I have also discovered that the bee communicates the advent of an enemy to the swarm. It was this dance which I performed, and the swarm attacked the indicated enemy, the Zu-Vendis. The dance movements are intricate, and certain polarisations of light play a necessary part in the message. These I simulated with my magnifying glass. But come, Watson, let us get our clothes on and be off before the swarm returns! I do not think I can pull that trick again. We do not want to be the game afoot."

We got the duke to his feet and half-carried him to the pass. Though he recovered consciousness, he seemed to have reverted to a totally savage state. He did not attack us but he regarded us suspiciously and made threatening growls if we got too close. We were at a loss to explain this frightening change in him. The frightening part came not so much from any danger he represented as from the dangers he was supposed to save us from. We had depended upon him to guide us and to feed and protect us on the way back. Without him even the incomparable Holmes was lost.

Fortunately, the duke recovered the next day and provided the explanation himself.

"For some reason I seem to be prone to receiving blows on the head," he said. "I have a thick skull, but every once in a while I get such a blow that even its walls cannot withstand the force. Sometimes, say about one out of three times, a complete amnesia results. I then revert to the state in which I was before I encountered white people. I am once again the uncivilised apeman; I have no memory of anything that occurred before I was twenty years old. This state may last for only a day, as you have seen, or it may persist for months."

"I would venture to say," Holmes said, "that this readiness to forget your contact with civilised peoples indicates an unconscious desire to avoid them. You are happiest when in the jungle and with no obligations. Hence your unconscious seizes upon every opportunity, such as a blow on the head, to go back to the happy primal time."

"Perhaps you are right," the duke said. "Now that my wife is dead, I would like to forget civilisation even exists. But I must see my country through this war first."

It took less than a month for us to get to Nairobi. Greystoke took excellent care of us, even though he was impatient to get back into action against the Germans. During the journey I had ample time to teach Nylepthah English and to get well acquainted with her. Before we reached the Lake Victoria railhead, I had proposed to her and been accepted. I will never forget that night. The moon was bright, and a hyena was laughing nearby.

The day before we reached the railhead, Greystoke went up a tree to check out the territory. A branch broke under his feet, and he landed on his head. When he regained consciousness, he was again the apeman. We could not come near him without his baring his teeth and growling menacingly. And that night he disappeared.

Holmes was very downcast by this. "What if he never gets over his amnesia, Watson? Then we will be cheated out of our fees."

"My dear Holmes," I said, somewhat coolly, "we never earned the fee in the first place. Actually, we were allowing ourselves to be bribed by the duke to keep silent."

"You never did understand the subtle interplay of economics and ethics," Holmes replied.

"There goes Von Bork," I said, glad to change the subject. I pointed to the fellow, who was sprinting across the veldt as if a lion were after him.

"He is mad if he thinks he can make his way alone to German East Africa," Holmes said. "But we must go after him! He has on him the formula for the SB."

"Where?" I asked for the hundredth time. "We have stripped him a dozen times and gone over every inch of his clothes and his skin. We have looked into his mouth and up…"

At that moment I observed Von Bork turn his head to the right to look at a rhinoceros which had come around a tall termite hill. The next moment, he had run the left side of his head and body into an acacia tree with such force that he bounced back several feet. He did not get up, which was just as well. The rhinoceros was looking for him and would have detected any movement by Von Bork. After prancing around and sniffing the air in several directions, the weak-eyed beast trotted off. Holmes and I hastened to Von Bork before he got his senses back and ran off once more.

"I believe I now know where the formula is," Holmes said.

"And how could you know that?" I said, for the thousandth time since I had first met him.

"I will bet my fee against yours that I can show you the formula within the next two minutes," he said, but I did not reply.

He kneeled down beside the German, who was lying on his back, his mouth and his eyes open. His pulse, however, beat strongly.

Holmes placed the tips of his thumbs under Von Bork's left eye. I stared aghast as the eye popped out.

"It's glass, Watson," Holmes said. "I had suspected that for some time, but I saw no reason to verify my suspicions until he was in a British prison. I was certain that his vision was limited to his right side when I saw him run into that tree. Even with his head turned away he would have seen it if his left eye had been effective."

He rotated the glass eye between thumb and finger while examining it through the magnifying glass. "Aha!" he exclaimed and then, handing the eye and glass to me, said, "See for yourself, Watson."

"Why," I said, "what I had thought were massive haemorrhages due to eye injury are tiny red lines of chemical formulae on the surface of the glass—if it *is* glass, and not some special material prepared to receive inscriptions."

"Very good, Watson," Holmes said. "Undoubtedly, Von Bork did not merely receive an injury to the eye in that motor-car crash of which

I heard rumours. He lost it, but the wily fellow had it replaced with an artificial eye which had more uses than—ahem—met the eye.

"After stealing the SB formula, he inscribed the surface of this false organ with the symbols. These, except through a magnifier, look like the results of dissipation or of an accident. He must have been laughing at us when we examined him so thoroughly, but he will laugh no more."

He took the eye back and pocketed it. "Well, Watson, let us rouse him from whatever dreams he is indulging in and get him into the proper hands. This time he shall pay the penalty for espionage."

Two months later we were back in England. We travelled by water, despite the danger of U-boats, since Holmes had sworn never again to get into an aircraft of any type. He was in a bad humour throughout the voyage. He was certain that Greystoke, even if he recovered his memory, would not send the promised cheques.

He turned the glass eye over to Mycroft, who sent it on to his superiors. That was the last we ever heard of it, and since the SB was never used, I surmise that the War Office decided that it would be too horrible a weapon. I was happy about this, since it just did not seem British to wage germ warfare. I have often wondered, though, what would have happened if Von Bork's mission had been successful. Would the Kaiser have countenanced SB as a weapon against his English cousins?

There were still three years of war to get through. I found lodgings for my wife and myself, and, despite the terrible conditions, the air raids, the food and material shortages, the dismaying reports from the front, we managed to be happy. In 1917 Nylepthah did what none of my previous wives had ever done. She presented me with a son. I was delirious with joy, even though I had to endure much joshing from my colleagues about fatherhood at my age. I did not inform

Holmes of the baby. I dreaded his sarcastic remarks.

On November 11, 1919, however, a year after the news that turned the entire Allied world into a carnival of happiness, though a brief one, I received a wire.

"Bringing a bottle and cigars to celebrate the good tidings. Holmes."

I naturally assumed that he referred to the anniversary of the Armistice. My surprise was indeed great when he showed up not only with the bottle of Scotch and a box of Havanas but a bundle of new clothes and toys for the baby and a box of chocolates for Nylepthah. The latter was a rarity at this time and must have cost Holmes some time and money to obtain.

"Tut, tut, my dear fellow," he said when I tried to express my thanks. "I've known for some time that you were the proud father. I have always intended to show up and tender my respects to the aged, but still energetic, father and to the beautiful Mrs. Watson. Never mind waking the infant up to show him to me, Watson. All babies look alike, and I will take your word for it that he is beautiful."

"You are certainly jovial," I said. "I do not ever remember seeing you more so."

"With good reason, Watson, with good reason!"

He dipped his hand into his pocket and brought out a cheque.

I looked at it and almost staggered. It was made out to me for the sum of thirty thousand pounds.

"I had given up on Greystoke," he said. "I heard that he was missing, lost somewhere in deepest Africa, probably dead. It seems, however, that he had found his wife was alive after all, and he was tracking her into the jungles of the Belgian Congo. He found her but was taken prisoner by some rather peculiar tribe. Eventually, his adopted son, you know, the Lt. Drummond who was to fly us to Marseilles, went after him and rescued his parents. And so, my dear fellow, one of the first things the duke did was to send the cheques! Both in my care, of course!"

"I can certainly use it," I said. "This will enable me to retire instead of working until I am eighty."

I poured two drinks for us and we toasted our good fortune. Holmes sat back in the chair, puffing upon the excellent Havana and watching Mrs. Watson bustle about her housework.

"She won't allow me to hire a maid," I said. "She insists on doing all the work, including the cooking, herself. Except for the baby and myself, she does not like to touch anyone or be touched by anyone. Sometimes I think…"

"Then she has shut herself off from all but you and the baby," he said.

"You might say that," I replied. "She is happy, though, and that is what matters."

Holmes took out a small notebook and began making notes in it. He would look up at Nylepthah, watch her for a minute, and record something.

"What are you doing, Holmes?" I said.

His answer showed me that he, too, could indulge in a pawky humour when his spirits were high.

"I am making some observations uopn the segregation of the queen."

THE END

Editor's Comments:

The reference on page 31 to the speed of the Handley Page was really in knots, not miles per hour. The editor has converted this to make it more intelligible to the reader.

The use of the word "queer" by Mycroft on page 26 has been criticised as not being realistic. Some Sherlockians have maintained that an Englishman in 1916 would not have known the word in its referent of "homosexual." However, that is the word Watson uses when he quotes Mycroft. So we must believe that some Englishmen, at least, were aware of this American term. Or, possibly, Watson's memory of the conversation was faulty. Since Watson had spent some time in the States, and had, like Holmes, picked up some Americanisms, he may have used this word because it was part of his everyday vocabulary.

The vulgarism, "a*****e," on page 41, needs one more asterisk. That is, it does if Watson was quoting the English term, which Holmes probably did utter. If Holmes was using the American word because he was speaking about an American, then the number of asterisks is accurate. We'll never know.

Afterword

BY WIN SCOTT ECKERT

S herlock Holmes lives!

Or at least he still might live, as Philip José Farmer points out in his Foreword to *The Peerless Peer*, noting that there is no record of the Great Detective's death. Farmer observes that the idea that Holmes lived, and still lives, thrives with an almost "religious belief" among his followers. Farmer slyly omits that he's one of the true believers, but it's clear he is.

It is fortunate indeed that Watson's manuscript survived. As Farmer relates, the good doctor's battered tin dispatch-box had been removed from the vaults of the bank of Cox and Co. at Charing Cross before the bank was bombed in World War II. It was stored for a time in Holmes' cottage near the village of Fulworth on the Sussex Downs, and thereafter, in the 1950s, came into the possession of the seventeenth Duke of Denver.

As everyone knows, the seventeenth Duke was better known as Lord Peter Wimsey, also an amateur detective of no little note, and a distant relative of Holmes. Lord Peter's cases were chronicled in a series of novels and short stories by Dorothy L. Sayers.

In 1973, the Duke of Denver authorized Farmer to edit Watson's manuscript for publication, and *The Adventure of the Peerless Peer* saw print the following year in a limited edition from Aspen Press. The Dell mass market paperback was issued in 1976, at which point we may suppose that Farmer was contacted by the Jungle Lord. As I've noted elsewhere,[1] Farmer had been under some pressure from the Ape-Man since the publication of his biography *Tarzan Alive* (Doubleday, 1972).

Farmer already knew of the Jungle Lord's deception (described in *The Peerless Peer*), or deduced it, based on his "An Exclusive Interview with Lord Greystoke" which took place on September 1, 1970. Or else he knew it from the extensive research which formed the basis of his *Tarzan Alive: A Definitive Biography of Lord Greystoke.* Or both. At that time, the Ape-Man persuaded Mr. Farmer to suppress certain details, such as his impersonation of his late cousin.

In 1974, when Watson's lost *Peerless Peer* manuscript was released and revealed that Sherlock Holmes had discovered the impersonation back in 1916, the Ape Lord was apparently not overly concerned. Perhaps an expensive and limited edition hardcover novel was not perceived as harmful. In addition, in late 1974, the Lord of the Jungle authorized Farmer to edit and publish memoirs in which he freely admitted to the deception ("Extracts from the Memoirs of 'Lord Greystoke,'" *Mother Was a Lovely Beast,* Philip José Farmer, ed., Chilton, 1974; *Tarzan Alive,* Bison Books, 2006).

However, the 1976 Dell paperback, inexpensive and widely available, was another matter altogether. The Lord of the Jungle, acting through a series of trusted middlemen, used his influence

---

1 *The Evil In Pemberley House*, Philip José Farmer and Win Scott Eckert, Subterranean Press, 2009.

to have the book suppressed. Farmer received a friendly warning letter from the Jungle Lord, now residing in parts unknown under an assumed name. (Farmer was not surprised at this, since the Ape-Man had indicated in their 1970 interview that he would soon fake his death and disappear.) The Jungle Lord had had enough of Farmer exposing his secrets to the public at large. Presumably he also wasn't terribly pleased with his fellow Duke, Lord Peter, for making Watson's manuscript available in the first place.

It can hardly matter, some thirty-five years later, if the truth about the Jungle Lord's impersonation is noted here, especially in light of the fact that the Ape-Man was not entirely successful in suppressing *The Peerless Peer* back in 1976; that he himself admitted it in his "Memoirs"; and that he approved of its recent republication in the collection *Venus on the Half-Shell and Others* (Christopher Paul Carey, ed., Subterranean Press, 2008).

Nonetheless, Farmer must have remained somewhat abashed by the Jungle Lord's rebuke. Perhaps he was also a bit sensitive to the Jungle Lord's constantly shifting positions on the matter. For his collection *The Grand Adventure* (Berkley Books, 1984), Farmer rewrote *The Peerless Peer* as the novella "The Adventure of the Three Madmen," replacing the Ape Lord with Rudyard Kipling's Mowgli. In his introduction to the rewrite, Farmer claimed that he had abandoned the pretense that Watson had written the original manuscript and that he (Farmer) was merely the editor. Now Farmer "admitted" that he was the "true author" of "Madmen." In fact, the reverse was true; he was using misdirection to cover for his former indiscretions.[2]

---

2 Interestingly, both *Peer* and "Madmen" may have been different drafts written by Watson, and each manuscript may contain large elements of the truth, despite the replacement of the Jungle Lord in *Peer* by Mowgli in "Madmen." Dennis E. Power has reconciled the two manuscripts in "Jungle Brothers, or, Secrets of the Jungle Lords," *Myths for the Modern Age: Philip José Farmer's Wold Newton Universe*, Win Scott Eckert, ed., MonkeyBrain Books, 2005.

By 2008, the Lord of the Jungle and his family had long-since faked their deaths, and the secrets revealed in *The Peerless Peer* were ancient enough history to cause no harm to the nobleman and his relations.[3] The novel was reprinted—once again in a limited edition.[4] Now, for the first time in thirty-five years, Watson's account is widely available in this new trade edition from Titan Books.

Sherlock Holmes, in the course of his lengthy career, encountered Count Dracula (numerous times), Doctor Who, Allan Quatermain, Arsène Lupin, Professor Challenger, the Phantom of the Opera, Raffles, Doctor Fu Manchu, Fantômas, the Time Traveller, Carnacki the Ghost-Finder, the Invisible Man, Father Brown, Doctor Jekyll and Mr. Hyde, Hercule Poirot, Sexton Blake, Harry Dickson, the Domino Lady, the Men from U.N.C.L.E., various Lovecraftian menaces, and The Batman (to name but a few noteworthy crossovers). He even battled the Martian Invaders.

And of course, in the case recorded as *The Peerless Peer*, he met that feral nobleman raised by "great apes."

But when Farmer edited Watson's account, it became clear that this exploit was not a mere crossover between two great men of their time. Holmes and Watson also ran into many other important personages during the events chronicled in *The Peerless Peer*.

One of Holmes and Watson's fliers in *Peer* is "Colonel Kentov." Kentov would later be known as the pulp vigilante The Shadow. In the pulp novel *The Shadow Unmasks*, it was revealed that The Shadow's real identity was that of aviator Kent Allard. Allard had also flown, and worked as a secret agent, for the Tsar during the Great War. During ·

---

3 In fact, the Ape-Man's ire had significantly cooled by the late 1990s, enough to allow Farmer to write an authorized entry in the series of semi-biographical novels covering his adventures. Farmer's *The Dark Heart of Time: A Tarzan Novel* was published by Del Rey Books in 1999.

4 It appeared in the aforementioned collection *Venus on the Half-Shell and Others*.

that time he had also been known as the Black Eagle and the Dark Eagle. As Farmer points out, one of The Shadow's many aliases during the 1930s and '40s was Lamont Cranston.

It's also worth noting that Holmes and Watson are conducted to Colonel Kentov's plane by a young Russian officer, Lieutenant Obrenov. In 1946, Farmer had chronicled a rather amusing World War II incident in Germany between a Colonel Obrenov and a U.S. officer, Colonel O'Brien.[5] Lieutenant Obrenov is killed in *The Peerless Peer*, but the Colonel is undoubtedly a relative.

When Holmes and Watson meet with Mycroft, the latter introduces young Henry Merrivale, who works at Military Intelligence and is quite accomplished in the art of detection. Sir Henry Merrivale went on to solve many mysteries from the 1930s through the 1950s. These cases were recounted by "Carter Dickson" (a pseudonym for John Dickson Carr).

Just before Mycroft summons him, Doctor Watson is sharing a brandy with a young friend, Doctor Fell. Doctor Fell is Gideon Fell, who would also go on to a lengthy career as an amateur detective from the 1930s through the 1960s. His cases were also recorded by John Dickson Carr.

Those familiar with American pulp magazines might think that the hallucinating pilot Wentworth is Richard Wentworth, who would later fight supercriminals in Manhattan as The Spider. However, Farmer notes that this mentally disturbed flyer, while in British service, used his half-brother's surname. Following Farmer's genealogical researches in *Doc Savage: His Apocalyptic Life* (revised edition, Bantam Books, 1975), this makes the crazed pilot G-8, the Great War hero whose exploits were related by Robert J. Hogan in the purple prose

---

5 "O'Brien And Obrenov," Adventure, V. 115, N. 5, March 1946; *Pearls from Peoria*, Paul Spiteri, ed., Subterranean Press, 2006.

pulp pages of *G-8 and His Battle Aces*. In fact, Farmer's researches revealed that G-8 and The Shadow were full brothers, and their half-brother was The Spider.

Leftenant John Drummond is mentioned as the adopted son of the Jungle Lord. This lines up with Farmer's discovery, documented in the biography *Tarzan Alive*, that the Ape-Man had an adopted son as well as a biological son. This discovery explains a severe chronological discrepancy in the original novels about the Jungle Lord, in which his son ages ten or eleven years, seemingly overnight, between the third and fourth novels.

Watson mentions Lord John Roxton, referring to him as being "wilder than the Amazon Indians with whom he consorted." Roxton accompanied Professor George Edward Challenger on the latter's expedition to the Lost World, in an account written by Edward Malone and edited for publication by Sir Arthur Conan Doyle.

The Jungle Lord, Holmes, and Watson locate the lost land of Zu-Vendis, last visited by Allan Quatermain, Sir Henry Curtis, Captain John Good, and the Zulu warrior Umslopogaas. Quatermain's Zu-Vendis adventure was recounted in *Allan Quatermain*, edited and published in 1887 by Sir Henry Rider Haggard, Quatermain's editor and biographer.

Farmer also realized that Watson's manuscript substantiated some of the genealogical researches he had conducted when writing the biographies *Tarzan Alive* and *Doc Savage: His Apocalyptic Life* (Doubleday, 1973; revised edition Bantam Books, 1975). Farmer had discovered that the subjects of these biographies were related to each other, and that both were related to many other heroes and villains whose exploits had been fictionalized in novels and short stories by various authors over the years. The almost superhuman nature of these personages' abilities was traced back to their ancestors' exposure to the ionized radiation of a meteorite which landed in the village of Wold Newton on December 13, 1795. Fitzwilliam Darcy and Elizabeth Bennet (whose story Jane Austen recounted in *Pride and Prejudice*) and Sir Percy Blakeney (also known as the Scarlet Pimpernel, whose tales were told by Baroness Emmuska Orczy) were among those present at the Wold Newton meteor strike.

The extensive group of related heroes, detectives, explorers, and villains came to be known as "the Wold Newton Family." Clearly, *The Peerless Peer* has a place as one of the primary books in Wold Newton mythos. How could it not, when Sherlock Holmes, Mycroft Holmes, the Jungle Lord, Leftenant Drummond, The Shadow, G-8, Lord John Roxton, and Allan Quatermain are all members of this extended family?

In addition to these, other members of the Wold Newton Family include Solomon Kane (a pre-meteor strike ancestor); Captain Blood (a pre-meteor strike ancestor); Professor Moriarty (aka Captain Nemo); Monsieur Lecoq; Phileas Fogg; the Time Traveller; Rudolf Rassendyll; A. J. Raffles; Wolf Larsen; Professor Challenger; Arsène Lupin; Richard Hannay; Bulldog Drummond; Doctor Fu Manchu and his nemesis Sir Denis Nayland Smith; Joseph Jorkens; Sam Spade; The Spider; Nero Wolfe; Mr. Moto; The Avenger; Philip Marlowe; James Bond; Lew Archer; Kilgore Trout; Travis McGee; and many more.

There are some other references in *The Peerless Peer* which solidify it as one of the foremost entries in the Wold Newton series. Watson's accidental reference to the sixth Duke of "Holdernesse" (rather than "Greystoke") makes it clear that story is tied to Holmes' previous case, "The Adventure of the Priory School." In *Tarzan Alive* and *Doc Savage*, Farmer's reveals that the great-nephew of the sixth Duke from "Priory School" is none other than the Ape Lord himself. And the sixth Duke's bastard son is the father of pulp hero Doc Savage.

Furthermore, "Holdernesse Hall" is actually Pemberley House, from *Pride and Prejudice*.

The biggest mystery that Holmes solves in *The Peerless Peer* is that of the Jungle Lord himself. He was legitimately the eighth Duke, but in order to avoid publicity surrounding his "feral man" status, he chose to pretend to be the seventh Duke, his late cousin, whom he greatly resembled. (This becomes a major plot point in Farmer's and my subsequent Wold Newton novel, *The Evil in Pemberley House*.)

At this stage a recounting of the ducal relationships is in order. The fifth Duke and the sixth Duke were brothers. The seventh Duke was the son of the sixth Duke. The Jungle Lord's father was the son of the fifth Duke, but he died before the fifth Duke. Therefore, when the fifth Duke died, the title passed to the fifth Duke's brother. The Jungle Lord was the grandson of the fifth Duke, and thus was the great-nephew of the sixth Duke. Leftenant John Drummond, the Jungle Lord's adopted son in *The Peerless Peer*, was therefore the great-great nephew of the sixth Duke. To put it another way, the sixth Duke was Drummond's great-great-uncle.

Early in *The Peerless Peer*, Mycroft reminds Sherlock that he (Sherlock) knew Leftenant Drummond's great-uncle, the late Duke (referring to the sixth Duke from Watson's "The Adventure of the Priory School").

When Mycroft makes this statement, everyone believes that the current duke is the seventh Duke, because the Jungle Lord, the legitimate eighth Duke, is posing as the late seventh Duke (no one knows that the seventh Duke has died). Therefore, since Leftenant John Drummond is described as the adopted son of the current (seventh) Duke, Mycroft should have reminded Sherlock that he (Sherlock) knew the Leftenant's *grandfather*, the late sixth Duke.

But he didn't.

Mycroft describes the late sixth Duke as Drummond's great-uncle, which is very close to the real relationship as Drummond's great-great-uncle. Despite Mycroft's usual precision, one might overlook this slight mistake, presuming that "great-great-uncle" could be shortened in conversation to "great-uncle."

However, Mycroft's description of the sixth Duke as Drummond's great-uncle demonstrates that he knew the truth of the Jungle Lord's deception and impersonation from the beginning. One can make a mistake or shorten "great-great-uncle" to "great-uncle." One doesn't make the mistake of saying "great-uncle" when one means "grandfather"–especially when one is Mycroft Holmes.

Mycroft already knew–*before* he sent Holmes and Watson on their African adventure–that the Ape-Man's cousin, the seventh Duke, had died, and that the Jungle Lord, the legitimate eighth Duke, had taken his late cousin's identity.

The story of how Mycroft came upon that knowledge is undoubtedly a fascinating one.

This revelation also raises the distinct possibility that Mycroft knew, when he sent Holmes and Watson on their aerial trek to Cairo to capture Von Bork, that they could well be blown off course by an impending "storm of the century," thus calling into question the coincidental nature of their meeting with the Lord of the Jungle.

But that's another story from the battered tin dispatch-box.

Win Scott Eckert
Denver, Colorado
March 2011

Coming Soon

MORIARTY

THE HOUND OF THE D'URBERVILLES

KIM NEWMAN

A Volume in Vermillion

I

I BLAME THAT RAT-WEASEL STAMFORD, who was no better at judging character than at kiting paper. He later had his collar felt in Farnham, of all blasted places. If you want to pass French government bonds, you can't afford to mix up your accents grave and your accents acute. Archie Stamford earns no sympathy from me. Thanks to him, I was first drawn into the orbit, the gravitational pull as he would have said, of Professor James Moriarty.

In 1880, your humble narrator was a vigorous, if scarred forty. I should make a proper introduction of myself: Colonel Sebastian 'Basher' Moran, late of a school which wouldn't let in an oik like you and a regiment which would as soon sack Newcastle as take Ali Masjid. I had an unrivalled bag of big cats and a fund of stories about blasting the roaring pests. I'd stood in the Khyber Pass and faced a surge of sword-waving Pathans howling for British blood, potting them like grouse in season. Nothing gladdens a proper Englishman's heart—this one, at least—like the sight of a foreigner's head flying into a dozen bloody bits. I'd dangled by single-handed grip from an icy ledge in the upper Himalayas, with something huge and indistinct and furry stamping on my freezing fingers. I'd bent like an oak in a hurricane as Sir Augustus, the hated pater, spouted paragraphs of bile in my face, which boiled down to the proverbial 'cut off without a penny' business. Stuck to it too, the mean old swine. The family loot went to a society for providing Christian undergarments to the Ashanti, a bequest which had the delightful side-effect of reducing my unmarriageable sisters to boarding-house penury.

I'd taken a dagger in the lower back from a harlot in Hyderabad and a pistol-ball in the knee from the Okhrana in Nijni-Novgorod. More to the point, I had recently been raked across the chest by the mad, wily old she-tiger the hill-heathens called 'Kali's Kitten'.

None of that was preparation for Moriarty!

I had crawled into a drain after the tiger, whose wounds turned out to be less severe than I'd thought. Tough old hell-cat! KK got playful with jaws and paws, crunching down my pith helmet like one of Carter's Little Liver Pills, delicately shredding my shirt with razor-claws, digging into the skin and drawing casually across my chest. Three bloody stripes. Sure I would die in that stinking tunnel, I was determined not to die alone. I got my Webley side-arm unholstered and shot the hell-bitch through the heart. To make sure, I emptied all six chambers. After that chit in Hyderabad dirked me, I broke her nose for her. KK looked almost as aghast and infuriated at being killed. I wondered if girl and tigress were related. I had the cat's rank dying breath in my face and her weight on me in that stifling hole. One more for the trophy wall, I thought. Cat dead, Moran not: hurrah and victory!

But KK nearly murdered me after all. The stripes went septic. Good thing there's no earthly use for the male nipple, because I found myself down to just the one. Lots of grey stuff came out of me. So I was packed off back to England for proper doctoring. It occurred to me that a concerted effort had been made to boot me out of the sub-continent. I could think of a dozen reasons for that, and a dozen clods in stiff collars who'd be happier with me out of the picture. Maiden ladies who thought tigers ought to be patted on the head and given treats. And the husbands, fathers and sweethearts of non-maiden ladies. Not to mention the First Bangalore Pioneers, who didn't care to be reminded of their habit of cowering in ditches while Bloody Basher did three-fourths of their fighting for them.

Still, mustn't hold a grudge, what? Sods, the lot of them. And that's just the whites. As for the natives… well, let's not get started on them, shall we? We'd be here 'til next Tuesday.

For me, a long sea-cruise is normally an opportunity. There are always bored fellow-passengers and underworked officers knocking around with fat note-cases in their luggage. It's most satisfying to sit on deck playing solitaire until some booby suggests a few rounds of cards and, why just to make it spicier, perhaps some trifling, sixpence-a-trick element of wager. Give me two months on any ocean in the world, and I can fleece everyone aboard from the captain's lady to the bosun's second-best bum-boy, and leave each mark convinced that the ship is a nest of utter cheats with only Basher as the other honest hand in the game.

Usually, I embark *sans* sou and stroll down the gang-plank at the destination pockets a-jingle with the accumulated fortune of my fellow voyagers. I get a warm feeling from ambling through the docks, listening to clots explaining to the eager sorts who've turned up to greet them that, sadly, the moolah which would have saved the guano-grubbing business or bought the Bibles for the mission or paid for the wedding has gone astray on the high seas. This time, tragic to report, I was off sick, practically in quarantine. My nimble fingers were away from the pasteboards, employed mostly in scratching around the bandages while trying hard not to scratch the bandages themselves.

So, the upshot: Basher in London, out of funds. And the word was abroad. I was politely informed by a chinless receptionist at Claridge's that my usual suite of rooms was engaged and that, unfortunately, no alternative was available this being a busy wet February and all. If I hadn't pawned my horsewhip, it would have got some use. If there's any breed I despise more than natives, it's people who work in bloody hotels. Thieves, the lot of them, or, what's worse, sneaks and snitches. They talk among themselves, so it was no use trotting down the street and trying somewhere else.

I was on the point of wondering if I shouldn't risk the Bagatelle Club, where—frankly—you're not playing with amateurs. There's the peril of wasting a whole evening shuffling and betting with other sharps who a) can't be rooked so easily and b) are liable to be as cash-poor as oneself. Otherwise, it was a matter of beetling up and down Piccadilly all afternoon in the hope of spotting a ten-bob note in the gutter, or—if it came to it—dragging Farmer Giles into a side-street, splitting his head and lifting his poke. A come-down after Kali's Kitten, but needs must…

'It's "Basher" Moran, isn't it?' drawled someone, prompting me to raise my sights from the gutter. 'Still shooting anything that draws breath?'

'Archibald Stamford, Esquire. Still practising auntie's signature?'

I remembered Archie from some police cells in Islington. All charges dropped and apologies made, in my case. Being 'mentioned in despatches' carries weight with beaks, certainly more than the word of a tradesman in a celluloid collar you clean with india-rubber. Six months jug for the fumbling forger, though. He'd been pinched trying to make a withdrawal from a relative's bank account.

If clothes were anything to go by, Stamford had risen in his profession. Stick-pin and cane, dove-grey morning coat, curly-brimmed topper and good boots. His whole manner, with that patronising hale-fellow-snooks-to-you tone, suggested he was in funds—which made him my long-lost friend.

The Criterion was handy, so I suggested we repair to the Bar for drinks. The question of who paid for them would be settled when Archie was fuddle-headed from several whiskies. I fed him that shut-out-of-my-usual-suite line and considered a hard luck story trading on my status as hero of the Jowaki Campaign—though I doubted an inky-fingered felon would put much stock in far-flung tales of imperial daring.

Stamford's eyes shone, in a manner which reminded me unpleasantly of my late feline dancing partner. He sucked on his teeth, torn between saying something and keeping mum. It was a manner I would soon come to recognise as common to those in the employ of my soon-to-be benefactor.

'As it happens, Bash old chap, I know a billet that might suit you. Comfortable rooms in Conduit Street, above Mrs Halifax's establishment. You know Mrs H?'

'Used to keep a knocking-shop in Stepney? Arm-wrestler's biceps and an eight-inch tongue?'

'That's the one. She's West End now. Part of a combine, you might say. A thriving firm.'

'What she sells is always in demand.'

'True, but it's not just the whoring. There's other business. A man of vision, you might say, has done some thinking. About my line of trade, and Mrs Halifax's, and, as it were, yours.'

I was about at the end of my rope with Archie. He was talking in a familiar, insinuating, creeping-round-behind-you-with-a-cosh manner

I didn't like. Implying that I was a tradesman did little for my ruddy temper. I was strongly tempted to give him one of my speciality thumps, which involves a neat little screw of my big fat regimental ring into the old eyeball, and see how his dove-grey coat looked with dirty great blobs of snotty blood down the front. After that, a quick fist into his waistcoat would leave him gasping, and give me the chance to fetch away his watch and chain, plus any cash he had on him. Of course, I'd check the spelling of 'Bank of England' on the notes before spending them. I could make it look like a difference of opinion between gentlemen. And no worries about it coming back to me. Stamford wouldn't squeal to the peelers. If he wanted to pursue the matter I could always give him a second helping.

'I wouldn't,' he said, as if he could read my mind.

That was a dash of Himalayan melt-water to the face.

Catching sight of myself in the long mirror behind the bar, I saw my cheeks had gone a nasty shade of red. More vermillion than crimson. My fists were knotted, white-knuckled, around the rail. This, I understand, is what I look like before I 'go off'. You can't live through all I have without 'going off' from time to time. Usually, I 'come to' in handcuffs between policemen with black eyes. The other fellow or fellows or lady is too busy being carried away to hospital to press charges.

Still, a 'tell' is a handicap for a card-player. And my red face gave warning.

Stamford smiled like someone who knows there's a confederate behind the curtain with a bead drawn on the back of your neck and a finger on the trigger.

Liberté, hah!

'Have you popped your guns, Colonel?'

I would pawn, and indeed have pawned, the family silver. I'd raise money on my medals, ponce my sisters (not that anyone would pay for the hymn-singing old trouts) and sell Royal Navy torpedo plans to the Russians... but a man's guns are sacred. Mine were at the Anglo-Indian Club, oiled and wrapped and packed away in cherrywood cases, along with a kit-bag full of assorted cartridges. If any cats got out of Regent's Park Zoo, I'd be well set up to use a Hansom for a howdah and track them along Oxford Street.

Stamford knew from my look what an outrage he had suggested. This wasn't the red-hot pillar-box-faced Basher bearing down on him, this was the deadly icy calm of—and other folks have said this, so it's not just me boasting—'the best heavy game shot that our Eastern Empire has produced'.

'There's a fellow,' he continued, nervously, 'this man of vision I mentioned. In a roundabout way, he is my employer. Probably the employer of half the folk in this room, whether they know it or not...'

He looked about. It was the usual shower: idlers and painted dames, jostling each other with stuck-on smiles, reaching sticky fingers into jacket-pockets and up loose skirts, finely-dressed fellows talking of 'business' which was no more than powdered thievery, a scattering of moon-faced cretins who didn't know their size-thirteens gave them away as undercover detectives.

Stamford produced a card and handed it to me.

'He's looking for a shooter...'

The fellow could never say the right thing. I am a sportsman, not a keeper. A gun, not a gunslinger. A shot, not a shooter.

Still, game is game...

'...and you might find him interesting.'

I looked down at the card. It bore the legend 'Professor James Moriarty', and an address in Conduit Street.

'A professor, is it?' I sneered. I pictured a dusty coot like the stick-men who'd bedevilled me through Eton (interminably) and Oxford (briefly). Or else a music-hall slickster, inflating himself with made-up titles. 'What might he profess, Archie?'

Stamford was a touch offended, and took back the card. It was as if Archie were a new convert to Popism and I'd farted during a sermon from Cardinal Newman.

'You've been out of England a long time, Basher.'

He summoned the barman, who had been eyeing us with that fakir's trick of knowing who was most likely, fine clothes or not, to do a runner.

'Will you be paying now, sirs?'

Stamford held up the card and shoved it in the man's face.

The barman went pale, dug into his own pocket to settle the tab, apologised, and backed off in terror.

Stamford just looked smug as he handed the card back to me.

II

‘

‘YOU HAVE BEEN IN AFGHANISTAN, I perceive,’ said the Professor.

‘How the devil did you know that,’ I asked in astonishment.

His eyes caught mine. Cobra-eyes, they say. Large, clear, cold, grey and fascinating. I’ve met cobras, and they aren’t half as deadly—trust me. I imagine Moriarty left off tutoring because his pupils were too terrified to con their two-times table. I seemed to suffer his gaze for a full minute, though only a few seconds passed. It had been like that in the hug of Kali’s Kitten. I’d have sworn on a stack of well-thumbed copies of *The Pearl* that the mauling went on for an hour of pain, but the procedure was over inside thirty seconds. If I’d had a Webley on my hip, I might have shot the Professor in the heart on instinct—though it’s my guess bullets wouldn’t dare enter him. He had a queer unhealthy light about him. Not unhealthy in himself, but for everybody else.

Suddenly, pacing distractedly about the room, head wavering from side to side as if he had two-dozen extra flexible bones in his neck, he began to rattle off facts.

Facts about me.

'… you are retired from your regiment, resigning at the request of a superior to avoid the mutual disgrace of dishonourable discharge; you have suffered a serious injury at the claws of a beast, are fully-recovered physically, but worry your nerve might have gone; you are the son of a late Minster to Persia and have two sisters, your only living relatives beside a number of unacknowledged half-native illegitimates; you are addicted most of all to gambling, but also to sexual encounters, spirits, the murder of animals, and the fawning of a duped public; most of the time, you blunder through life like a bull, snatching and punching to get your own way, but in moments of extreme danger you are possessed by a strange serenity which has enabled you to survive situations that would have killed another man; in fact, your true addiction is to danger, to fear—only near death do you feel alive; you are unscrupulous, amoral, habitually violent and, at present, have no means of income, though your tastes and habits require a constant inflow of money…'

Throughout this performance, I took in Professor James Moriarty. Tall, stooped, hair thin at the temples, cheeks sunken, wearing a dusty (no, chalky) frock-coat, sallow as only an indoorsman can be, yellow cigarette-stain between his first and second fingers, teeth to match. And, obviously, very pleased with himself.

He reminded me of Gladstone gone wrong. With just a touch of a hill-chief who had tortured me with fire-ants.

But I had no patience with his lecture. I'd eaten enough of that from the pater for a lifetime.

'Tell me something I don't know,' I interrupted …

The Professor was unpleasantly surprised. It was as if no one had ever dared break into one of his speeches before. He halted in his tracks, swivelled his skull and levelled those shotgun-barrelhole eyes at me.

'I've had this done at a bazaar,' I continued. 'It's no great trick. The fortune-teller notices tiny little things and makes dead-eye guesses—you can tell I gamble from the marks on my cuffs, and was in Afghanistan by the colour of my tan. If you spout with enough confidence, you score so many hits the bits you get wrong—like that tommyrot about being addicted to danger—are swallowed and forgotten. I'd expected a better show from your advance notices, "Professor".'

He slapped me across the face, swiftly, with a hand like wet leather. Now, I was amazed.

I knew I was vermillion again, and my dukes went up.

Moriarty whirled, coat-tails flying, and his boot-toe struck me in the groin, belly and chest. I found myself sat in a deep chair, too shocked to hurt, pinned down by wiry, strong hands which pressed my wrists to the armrests. That dead face was close up to mine and those eyes horribly filled the view.

That calm he mentioned came on me. And I knew I should just sit still and listen.

'Only an idiot guesses or reasons or deduces,' the Professor said, patiently. He withdrew, which meant I could breathe again and become aware of how much pain I was in. 'No one comes into these rooms unless I know everything about him that can be found out through the simple means of asking behind his back. The public record is easily filled in by looking in any one of a number of reference books, from the *Army Guide* to *Who's Who*. But all the interesting material comes from a man's enemies. I am not a conjurer, Colonel Moran. I am a scientist.'

There was a large telescope in the room, aimed out of the window. On the walls were astronomical charts and a collection of impaled insects. A long side-table was piled with brass, copper and glass contraptions I took for parts of instruments used in the study of the stars or navigation at sea. That shows I wasn't yet used to the Professor. Everything about him was lethal, and that included his assorted bric-a-brac.

It was hard to miss the small kitten pinned to the mantel-piece by a jack-knife. The skewering had been skilfully done, through the velvety skin-folds of the haunches. The animal mewled from time to time, not in any especial pain.

'An experiment with morphine derivatives,' he explained. 'Tibbles will let us know when the effect wears off.'

Moriarty posed by his telescope, bony fingers gripping his lapel.

I remembered Stamford's manner, puffed up with a feeling he was protected but tinged with terror. At any moment, the great power to which he had sworn allegiance might capriciously or justifiably turn on him with destructive ferocity. I remembered the Criterion barman digging into his own pocket to settle our bill—which, I now realised, was as natural as the Duke of Clarence gumming his own stamps or Florence Nightingale giving sixpenny knee-tremblers in D'Arblay Street.

Beside the Professor, that ant-man was genteel.

'Who are you?' I asked, unaccustomed to the reverential tone I heard in my own voice. 'What are you?'

Moriarty smiled his adder's smile.

And I relaxed. I knew. My destiny and his wound together. It was a sensation I'd never got before upon meeting a man. When I'd had it from women, the upshot ranged from disappointment to attempted murder. Understand me, Professor James Moriarty was a hateful man, the most hateful, hateable, creature I have ever known, not excluding Sir Augustus and Kali's Kitten and the Abominable Bloody Snow-Bastard and the Reverend Henry James Prince[1]. He was something

---

1. Henry James Prince (1811-99), excommunicated from the Church of England for 'radical teachings', founded a pseudo-religious order, the Agapemone (Abode of Love), in Spaxton, Somerset, in 1845. His most fervent disciples were women with money. The Agapemone was one of several 19th century communions run along the lines of the cults later established by Sun Myung Moon or L. Ron Hubbard. The circumstances of Moran's encounter or encounters with Prince are not known at this time. See: The Reverend Prince and His Abode of Love (Charles Mander, EP Publishing, 1976).

man-shaped that had crawled out from under a rock and moved into the manor house. But, at that moment, I was his, and I remain his forever. If I am remembered, it will be because I knew him. From that day on, he was my father, my commanding officer, my heathen idol, my fortune and terror and rapture.

God, I could have done with a stiff drink.

Instead, the Professor tinkled a silly little bell and Mrs Halifax trotted in with a tray of tea. One look and I could tell she was his too. Stamford had understated the case when he said half the folk in the Criterion Bar worked for Moriarty. My guess is that, at bottom, the whole world works for him. They've called him the Napoleon of Crime, but that's just putting what he is, what he does, in a cage. He's not a criminal, he is crime itself, sin raised to an art-form, a church with no religion but rapine, a God of Evil. Pardon my purple prose, but there it is. Moriarty brings things out in people, things from their depths.

He poured me tea.

'I have had an eye on you for some time, Colonel Moran. Some little time. Your dossier is thick, in here…'

He tapped his concave temple.

This was literally true. He kept no notes, no files, no address-book or appointment-diary. It was all in his head. Someone who knows more than I do about sums told me that Moriarty's greatest feat was to write *The Dynamics of an Asteroid*, his magnum opus, in perfect first draft. From his mind to paper, with no preliminary notations or pencilled workings, never thinking forward to plan or skipping back to correct. As if he were singing 'one long, pure note of astro-mathematics, like a castrato nightingale delivering a hundred-thousand-word telegram from Prometheus.'

'You have come to these rooms and have already seen too much to leave…'

An ice-blade slid through my ribs into my heart.

'...except as, we might say, one of the family.'

The ice melted, and I felt tingly and warm. With the phrase, 'one of the family', he had arched his eyebrow invitingly.

He stroked Tibbles, who was starting to leak and make nasty little noises.

'We are a large family, many cells with no knowledge of each other, devoted to varied pursuits. Most, though not all, are concerned with money. I own that other elements of our enterprise interest me far more. We are alike in that. You only think you gamble for money. In fact, you gamble to lose. You even hunt to lose, knowing you must eventually be eaten by a predator more fearsome than yourself. For you, it is an emotional, instinctual, sensual thrill. For me, there are intellectual, aesthetic, spiritual rewards. But, inconveniently, money must come into it. A great deal of money.'

As I said, he had me sold already. If a great deal of money was to be had, Moran was in.

'The Firm is available for contract work. You understand? We have clients, who bring problems to us. We solve them, using whatever skills we have to hand. If there is advantage to us beyond the agreed fee, we seize it...'

He made a fist in the air, as if squeezing a microbe to death.

'...if our interests happen to run counter to those of the client, we settle the matter in such a way that we are ultimately convenienced while our patron does not realise precisely what has happened. This, also, you understand?'

'Too right, Professor,' I said.

'Good. I believe we shall have satisfaction of each other.'

I sipped my tea. Too milky, too pale. It always is after India. I think they put curry-powder in the pot out there, or else piddle in the sahib's crockery when he's not looking.

'Would you care for one of Mrs Halifax's biscuits?' he asked, as if he were the vicar entertaining the chairwoman of the beneficent fund. 'Vile things, but you might like them.'

I dunked and nibbled. Mrs H was a better madame than baker. Which led me to wonder what fancies might be buttered up in the rooms below the Professor's lair.

'Colonel Moran, I am appointing you as head of one of our most prestigious divisions. It is a post for which you are eminently qualified by achievement and aptitude. Technically, you are superior to all in the Firm. You are expected to take up residence here, in this building. A generous salary comes with the position. And profit participation in, ah, "special projects". One such matter is at hand, and we shall come to it when we receive our next caller, Mister–no, not Mister, Elder–Elder Enoch J. Drebber of Cleveland, Ohio.'

'I'm flattered,' I responded. 'A "generous salary" would solve my problems, not to mention the use of a London flat. But, Moriarty, what is this division you wish me to head? Why am I such a perfect fit for it? What, specifically, is its business?'

Moriarty smiled again.

'Did I omit to mention that?'

'You know damn well you did!'

'Murder, my dear Moran. Its business is murder.'

III

❦

BARELY TEN MINUTES AFTER MY APPOINTMENT as Chief Executive
Director of Homicide, Ltd., I was awaiting our first customer.

I mused humorously that I might offer an introductory special,
say a garrotting thrown in gratis with every five poisonings.
Perhaps there should be a half-rate for servants? A sliding scale
of fees, depending on the number of years a prospective victim
might reasonably expect to have lived had a client not retained our
services?

I wasn't yet thinking the Moriarty way. Hunting I knew to be a
serious avocation. Murder was for bounders and cosh-men, hardly
even killing at all. I'm not squeamish about taking human life:
Quakers don't get decorated after punitive actions against Afghan
tribesmen. But not one of the heap of unwashed heathens I'd laid in
the dust in the service of Queen and Empire had given me a quarter
the sport of the feeblest tiger I ever bagged.

Shows you how little I knew then.

The Professor chose not to receive Elder Drebber in his own rooms, but made use of the brothel parlour. The room was well supplied with plushly upholstered divans, laden at this early evening hour with plushly upholstered tarts. It occurred to me that my newfound position with the Firm might entitle me to handle the goods. I even took the trouble mentally to pick out two or three bints who looked ripe for what ladies the world over have come to know as the Basher Moran Special. Imagine the Charge of the Light Brigade between silk sheets, or over a dresser table, or in an alcove of a Ranee's Palace, or up the Old Kent Road, or... well, any place really.

As soon as I sat down, the whores paid attention, cooing and fluttering like doves, positioning themselves to their best advantage. As soon as the Professor walked in, the flock stood down, finding minute imperfections in fingernails or hair that needed rectifying.

Moriarty looked at the dollies and then at me, constructing something on his face that might have passed for a salacious, comradely leer but came out wrong. The bare-teeth grin of a chimpanzee, taken for a cheery smile by sentimental zoo visitors, is really a frustrated snarl of penned, homicidal fury. The Professor also had an alien range of expression, which others misinterpreted at their peril.

Mrs Halifax ushered in our American callers.

Enoch J. Drebber—why d'you think Yankees are so keen on those blasted middle initials?—was a barrel-shaped fellow, *sans* moustache but with a fringe of tight black curls all the way round his face. He wore simple, expensive black clothes and a look of stern disapproval.

The girls ignored him. I sensed he was on the point of fulminating.

I didn't need one of the Professor's 'background checks' to get Drebber's measure. He was one of those odd godly bods who get voluptuous pleasure from condemning the fleshly failings of others. As a Mormon, he could bag as many wives as he wanted—on-tap whores and unpaid skivvies corralled together. His right eye roamed around the room, on the scout for the eighth or ninth Mrs Drebber, while his left was fixed straight ahead at the Professor.

With him came a shifty cove by the name of Brother Stangerson who kept quiet but paid attention.

'Elder Drebber, I am Professor Moriarty. This is Colonel Sebastian Moran, late of the First Bangalore…'

Drebber coughed, interrupting the niceties.

'You're who to see in this city if a Higher Law is called for?'

Moriarty showed empty hands.

'A man must die, and that's the story,' said Drebber. 'He should have died in South Utah, years ago. He's a murderer, plain and flat, and an abductor of women. Hauled out his six-gun and shot Bishop Dyer, in front of the whole town. A crime against God. Then fetched away Jane Withersteen, a good Mormon woman, and her adopted child, Little Fay. He threw down a mountain on his pursuers, crushing Elder Tull and many good Mormon men[2] Took away gold that was rightful property of the Church, stole it right out of the ground. The Danite Band have been pursuing him ever since…'

'The Danites are a cabal within the Church of Latter-Day Saints,' explained Moriarty.

'God's good right hand is what we are,' insisted Drebber. 'When the laws of men fail, the unworthy must be smitten, as if by lightning.'

---

2. A more balanced account of these incidents can be found Riders of the Purple Sage (Zane Grey, Harper & Brothers, 1912).

I got the drift. The Danites were cossacks, assassins and vigilantes wrapped up in a Bible name. Churches, like nations, need secret police forces to keep the faithful in line.

'Who is this, ah, murderer and abductor?' I asked.

'His name, if such a fiend deserves a name, is Lassiter. Jim Lassiter.'

This was clearly supposed to get a reaction. The Professor kept his own council. I admitted I'd never heard of the fellow.

'Why, he's the fastest gun in the South-West. Around Cottonwoods, they said he struck like a serpent, drawing and discharging in one smooth, deadly motion. Men he killed were dead before they heard the sound of the shot. Lassiter could take a man's eye out at three hundred yards with a pistol.'

That's a fairy story. Take it from someone who knows shooting. A side-arm is handy for close-work, as when, for example, a tiger has her talons in your tit. With anything further away than a dozen yards, you might as well throw the gun as fire it.

I kept my scepticism to myself. The customer is always right, even in the murder business.

'This Lassiter,' I ventured. 'Where might he be found?'

'In this city,' Drebber decreed. 'We are here, ah, on the business of the Church. The Danites have many enemies, and each of us knows them all. I was half-expecting to come across another such pestilence, a cur named Jefferson Hope who need not concern you, but it was Lassiter I happened upon, walking in your Ly-cester Square on Sunday afternoon. I saw the Withersteen woman first, then the girl, chattering for hot chestnuts. I knew the apostate for who she was. She has been thrice condemned and outcast...'

'You said she was abducted,' put in the Professor. 'Now you imply she is with Lassiter of her own will?'

'He's a Devil of persuasion, to make a woman refuse an Elder of the Church and run off with a damned Gentile. She has no mind of her own, like all women, and cannot fully be blamed for her sins…'

If Drebber had a horde of wives around the house and still believed that, he was either very privileged or very unobservant.

'Still, she must be brought to heel. Though the girl will do as well. A warm body must be taken back to Utah, to come into an inheritance.'

'Cottonwoods,' said Moriarty. 'The ranch, the outlying farms, the cattle, the racehorses and, thanks to those inconveniently-upheld claims, the fabulous gold-mines of Surprise Valley.'

'The Withersteen property, indeed. When it was willed to her by her father, a great man, it was on the understanding she would become the wife of Elder Tull, and Cottonwoods would come into the Church. Were it not for this Lassiter, that would have been the situation.'

Profits, not parsons, were behind this.

'The Withersteen property will come to the girl, Fay, upon the death of the adoptive mother?'

'That is the case.'

'One or other of the females must be alive?'

'Indeed so.'

'Which would you prefer? The woman or the girl?'

'Jane Withersteen is the more steeped in sin, so there would be a certain justice…'

'…if she were topped too,' I finished his thought.

Elder Drebber wasn't comfortable with that, but nodded.

'Are these three going by their own names?'

'They are not,' said Drebber, happier to condemn enemies than contemplate his own schemes against them. 'This Lassiter has steeped his women in falsehood, making them bear repeated false witness, over and over. That such crimes should go unpunished is an offence to God Himself…'

'Yes, yes, yes,' I said. 'But what names are they using, and where do they live?'

Drebber was tugged out of his tirade, and thought hard.

'I caught only the false name of Little Fay. The Withersteen woman called her "Rache", doubtless a diminutive for the godly name "Rachel"…'

'Didn't you think to tail these, ah, varmints, to their lair?'

Drebber was offended. 'Lassiter is the best tracker the South West has ever birthed. Including Apaches. If I dogged him, he'd be on me faster'n a rattler on a coon.'

The Elder's vocabulary was mixed. Most of the time, he remembered to sound like a preacher working up a lather against sin and sodomy. When excited, he sprinkled in terms which showed him up for—in picturesque 'Wild West' terms—a back-shooting, claim-jumping, cow-rustling, waterhole-poisoning, horse-thieving, side-winding owlhoot son-of-a-bitch.

'Surely he thinks he's safe here and will be off his guard?'

'You don't know Lassiter.'

'No, and, sadly for us all, neither do you. At least, you don't know where he hangs his hat.'

Drebber was deflated.

Moriarty said 'Mr and Mrs James Lassiter and their daughter Fay currently reside at The Laurels, Streatham Hill Road, under the names Jonathan, Helen and Rachel Laurence.'

Drebber and I looked at the Professor. He had enjoyed showing off.

Even Stangerson clapped a hand to his sweaty forehead.

'Considering there's a fabulous gold mine at issue, I consider fifty thousand a fair price for contriving the death of Mr Laurence,' said Moriarty, as if putting a price on a fish supper. 'With an equal sum for his lady wife.'

Drebber nodded again, once. 'The girl comes with the package?'

'I think a further hundred thousand for her safekeeping, to be redeemed when we give her over into the charge of your church.'

'Another hundred thousand pounds?'

'Guineas, Elder Drebber.'

He thought about it, swallowed, and stuck out his paw.

'Deal, Professor…'

Moriarty regarded the American's hand. He turned and Mrs Halifax was beside him with a salver bearing a document.

'Such matters aren't settled with a handshake, Elder Drebber. Here is a contract, suitably circumlocutionary as to the nature of the services Colonel Moran will be performing, but meticulously exact in detailing payments entailed and the strict schedule upon which monies are to be transferred. It's legally binding, for what that's worth, but a contract with us is enforceable under what you have referred to as a Higher Law…'

The Professor stood by a lectern, which bore an open, explicitly-illustrated volume of the sort found in establishments like Mrs Halifax's for occasions when inspiration flags. He unrolled the document over a coloured plate, then plucked a pen from an inkwell and presented it to Drebber.

The Elder made a pretence of reading the rubric and signed.

Professor Moriarty pressed a signet-ring to the paper, impressing a stylised M below Drebber's dripping scrawl.

The document was whisked away.

'Good day, Elder Drebber.'

Moriarty dismissed the client, who backed out of the room.

'What are you waiting for?' I said to Stangerson, who stuck on the hat he had been fiddling with and scarpered.

One of the girls giggled at his departure, then remembered herself and pretended it was a hiccough. She paled under her rouge at the Professor's sidelong glance.

'Colonel Moran, have you given any thought to hunting a Lassiter?'

IV

A JUNGLE IS A JUNGLE, even if it's in Streatham and is made up of villas named after shrubs.

In my coat-pocket I had my Webley.

If I were one of those cowboys, I'd have notched the barrel after killing Kali's Kitten. Then again, even if I only counted white men and tigers, I didn't own any guns with a barrels long enough to keep score. A gentleman doesn't need to list his accomplishments or his debts, since there are always clerks to keep tally. I might not have turned out to be a pukka gent, but I was flogged and fagged at Eton beside future cabinet ministers and archbishops, and some skins you never shed.

It was bloody cold, as usual in London. Not raining, no fog—which is to say, no handy cover of darkness—but the ground chill rose through my boots and a nasty wind whipped my face like wet pampas grass.

The only people outside this afternoon were hurrying about their business with scarves around their ears, obviously part of the landscape.

I had decided to toddle down and poke around, as a preliminary to the business in hand. Call it a recce.

Before setting out, I'd had the benefit of a lecture from the Professor. He had devoted a great deal of thought to murder. He could have written the Baedeker's or Bradshaw's of the subject. It would probably have to be published anonymously—*A Complete Guide to Murder*, by 'A Distinguished Theorist'—and then be liable to seizure or suppression by the philistines of Scotland Yard.

'Of course, Moran, murder is the easiest of all crimes, if murder is all one has in mind. One simply presents one's card at the door of the intended victim, is ushered into his sitting room and blows his or, in these enlightened times her, brains out with a revolver. If one has omitted to bring along a firearm, a poker or candlestick will serve. Physiologically, it is not difficult to kill another person, to perform outrages upon a human corpus which will render it a human corpse. Strictly speaking, this is a successful murder. Of course, then comes the second, far more challenging part of the equation: getting away with it.'

I'd been stationed across the road from The Laurels for a quarter of an hour, concealed behind bushes, before I noticed I was in Streatham Hill Rise not Streatham Hill Road. This was another Laurels, with another set of residents. This was a boarding house for genteel folk of a certain age. I was annoyed enough, with myself and the locality, to consider potting the landlady just for the practice.

If I held the deeds to this district and the Black Hole of Calcutta, I'd live in the Black Hole and rent out Streatham. Not only was it beastly cold, but stultifyingly dull. Row upon monotonous row of The Lupins, The Laburnums, The Leilandii and The Laurels. No wonder I was in the wrong spot.

'It is a little-known fact that most murderers don't care about getting away with it. They are possessed by an emotion—at first, perhaps, a mild irritation about the trivial habit of a wife, mother, master or mistress. This develops over time, sprouting like a seed, to the point when only the death of another will bring peace. These murderers go happy to the gallows, free at last of their victim's clacking false teeth or unconscious chuckle or penny-pinching. We shun such as amateurs. They undertake the most profound action one human being can perform upon another, and fail to profit from the enterprise.'

No, I had not thought to purchase one of those penny-maps. Besides, anyone on the street with a map is obviously a stranger. Thus the sort who, after the fact, lodges in the mind of witnesses. 'Did you see anyone suspicious in the vicinity, Madam Busybody?' 'Why yes, Sergeant Flat-Foot, a lost-looking fellow, very red in the face, peering at street signs. Come to think of it, he looked like a murderer. And he was the very spit and image of that handsome devil whose picture was in the Illustrated Press after single-handedly seeing off the Afghan hordes that time.'

'Our business is murder for profit, killing for cash,' Moriarty had put it. 'We do not care about our clients' motives, providing they meet the price. They may wish murder to gain an inheritance, inflict revenge, make a political point or from sheer spite. In this case, all four conditions are in play. The Danite Band, represented by Elder Drebber, seek to secure the gold mine, avenge the deaths of their fellow conspirators, indicate to others who might defy them that they are dangerous to cross, and see dead a foeman they are not skilled enough to best by themselves.'

What was the use of a fanatical secret society if it couldn't send a horde of expendable minions to overwhelm the family? These Danite

Desperadoes weren't up there with the Thuggee or the Dacoits when it came to playing that game. If the cabal really sought to usurp the governance of their church, which the Professor confided they had in mind, a greater quantity of sand would be required.

'For centuries, the art of murder has stagnated. Edged weapons, blunt instruments and bare hands that would have served our ancient ancestors are still in use. Even poisons were perfected in classical times. Only in the last hundred and fifty years have fire-arms come to dominate the murder market-place. For the cruder assassin, the explosive device—whether planted or flung—has made a deal of noise, though at the expense of accuracy. Presently, guns and bombs are more suited to the indiscriminate slaughter of warfare or massacre than the precision of wilful murder. That, Moran, we must change. If guns can be silenced, if skills you have developed against big game can be employed in the science of man-slaying, then the field will be revolutionised.'

I beetled glumly up and down Streatham Hill.

'Imagine, if you will, a Minister of State or a Colossus of Finance or a Royal Courtesan, protected at all hours by professionals, beyond the reach of any would-be murderer, vulnerable only to the indiscriminate anarchist with his oh-so-inaccurate bomb and willingness to be a martyr to his cause. Then think of a man with a rifle, stationed at a window or on a balcony some distance from the target, with a telescopic device attached to his weapon, calmly drawing a bead and taking accurate, deadly shots. A sniper, Moran, as used in war, brought to bear in a civilian circumstance, a private enterprise. While guards panic around their fallen employer, in a tizzy because they don't even know where the shot has come from, our assassin packs up and strolls away untroubled, unseen and untraced. That will be the murder of the future, Moran. The scientific murder.'

Then the Professor rattled on about air-guns, which lost me. Only little boys and pouffes would deign to touch a contraption which needs to be pumped before use and goes off with a sad phut rather than a healthy bang. Kali's Kitten would have swallowed an air-gun whole and taken an arm along with it. The whiff of cordite, that's the stuff—better than cocaine any day of the month. And the big bass drum thunder of a gun going off.

Finally, I located the right Laurels.

Evening was coming on. Gaslight flared behind net-curtains. More shadows to slip in. I felt comfy, as if I had thick foliage around me. My ears pricked for the pad of a big cat. I found a nice big tree and leaned against it.

I took out an instrument Moriarty had issued from his personal collection, a spy-glass tricked up to look like a hip-flask. Off came the stopper and there was an eye-piece. Up to the old ocular as if too squiffy to crook the elbow with precision, and the bottom of the bottle was another lens. Brought a scene up close, in perfect, sharp focus.

Lovely bit of kit.

I saw into the front-parlour of the Laurels. A fire was going and the whole household was at home. A ripening girl, who wore puffs and ribbons more suited to the nursery, flounced around tiresomely. I saw her mouth flap, but—of course—couldn't hear what she was saying. A woman sat by the fire, nodding and doing needlework, occasionally flashing a tight smile. I focused on the chit, Fay-called-Rachel, then on the mother, Helen Laurence-alias-Jane Withersteen. I recalled the 'daughter' was adopted, and wondered what that was all about. The woman was no startler, with grey in her dark hair as if someone had cracked an egg over her head and let it run. The girl might do in a pinch. Looking again at her animated face, it hit me that she was feeble-witted.

The man, Jonathan Laurence-né-Jim Lassiter, had his back to the window. He seemed to be nodding stiffly, then I realised he was in a rocking chair. I twisted a screw and the magnification increased. I saw the back of his neck, tanned, and the sharp cut of his hair, slick with pomade. I even made out the ends of his moustache, wide enough to prick out either side of the silhouette of his head.

So this was the swiftest pistolero West of the Pecos?

I admit I snorted.

This American idiocy about drawing and firing, taking aim in a split-second, is stuff and nonsense. Anyone who wastes their time learning how to do conjuring tricks getting their gun out is likely to find great red holes in their shirt-front (or, in most cases, back) before they've executed their fanciest twirl. That's if they don't shoot their own nose off by mistake. Bill Hickock, Jesse James and Billy the Kid were all shot dead while unarmed or asleep by folk far less famous and skilled.

Dash it all, I was going to chance it. All I had to do was take out the Webley, cross the road, creep into the front garden, stand outside the window, and blast Mr and Mrs Laurence where they sat.

The fun part would be snatching the girl.

Carpe diem, they said at Eton. *Take your shot*, I learned in the jungle. Nothing ruddy ventured, nothing bloody gained.

I stoppered the spy-glass and slipped it into my breast-pocket. Using it had an odd side-effect. My mouth was dry and I really could have done with a swallow of something. But I had surrendered my proper hip-flask in exchange for the trick-telescope. I wouldn't make that mistake again. Perhaps Moriarty could whip me up a flask disguised as a pocket-watch. And, if time-keeping was important, a pocket-watch disguised as something I'd never need, like a prayer-book or a tin of fruit pastilles.

The girl was demonstrating some dance now. Really, I would do the couple a favour by getting them out of this performance.

I reached into my coat-pocket and gripped my Webley. I took it out slowly and carefully—no nose-ectomy shot for Basher Moran—and cocked it with my thumb. The sound was tinier than a click you'd make with your tongue against your teeth.

Suddenly, Lassiter wasn't in view. He was out of his chair and beyond sight of the window.

I was dumbfounded.

Then the lights went out. Not only the gas, but the fire—doused by a bucket, I'd guess. The womenfolk weren't in evidence, either.

One tiny click!

A finger stuck out from a curtain and tapped the window-pane.

No, not a finger. A tube. If I'd had the glass out, I could confirm what I intuited. The bump at the end of the tube was a sight. Lassiter, the fast gun, had drawn his iron.

I had fire in my belly. I smelled the dying breath of Kali's Kitten.

I changed my estimate of the American. What had seemed a disappointing, drab day outing was now a worthwhile safari, a game worth the chase.

He wouldn't come out of the front door, of course.

He needn't come out at all. First, he'd secure the mate and cub—a stronghold in the cellar, perhaps. Then he'd get a wall behind his back and wait. To be bearded in his lair. If only I had a bottle of paraffin, or even a box of matches. Then I could fire The Laurels: they'd have to come out and Lassiter would be distracted by females in panic. No, even then, there was a back-garden. I'd have needed beaters, perhaps a second and third gun.

Moriarty had said he could put reliable men at my disposal for the job, but I'd pooh-poohed the suggestion. Natives panic and run, lesser guns get in the way. I was best off on my tod.

I had to rethink. Lassiter was on his guard now. He could cut and run, spirit his baggages off with him. Go to ground so we'd never find him again.

My face burned. Suddenly I was afraid, not of the gunslinger, but of the Prof. I would have to tell him of my blunder.

One bloody click, that was all it was! Damn and drat.

I knew, even on brief acquaintance, Moriarty did not merely dismiss people from the Firm. He was no mere theoretician of murder.

Moran's head, stuffed, on Moriarty's wall. That would be the end of it.

I eased the cock of the Webley shut and pocketed the gun.

A cold circle pressed to the back of my neck.

'Reach, pardner,' said a deep, foreign, marrow-freezing voice. 'And mighty slow-like.'

Moriarty: The Hound of the D'Urbervilles
By Kim Newman

Available from Titan Books, September 2011

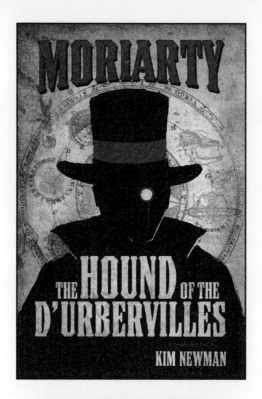

MORIARTY

THE HOUND OF THE D'URBERVILLES

Kim Newman

Imagine the twisted evil twins of Holmes and Watson and you have the dangerous
duo of Professor James Moriarty—wily, snake-like, fiercely intelligent, unpredictable
—and Colonel Sebastian 'Basher' Moran—violent, politically incorrect, debauched.
Together they run London crime, owning police and criminals alike. Unravelling
mysteries—all for their own gain.

ISBN: 9780857682833

AVAILABLE SEPTEMBER 2011

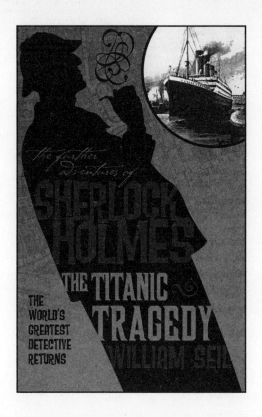

THE FURTHER ADVENTURES
OF SHERLOCK HOLMES
THE TITANIC TRAGEDY

William Seil

Sherlock Holmes and Dr. Watson board the Titanic in 1912, where Holmes is
to carry out a secret government mission. Soon after departure, highly important
submarine plans for the U.S. navy are stolen. Holmes and Watson work through a
list of suspects which includes Colonel James Moriarty, brother to the late Professor
Moriarty—will they find the culprit before tragedy strikes?

ISBN: 9780857687104

AVAILABLE MARCH 2012

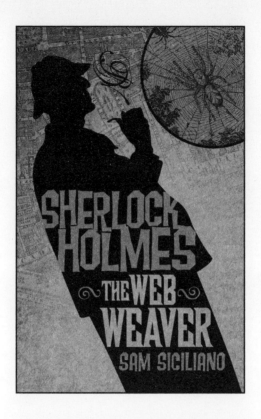

THE FURTHER ADVENTURES
OF SHERLOCK HOLMES

THE WEB WEAVER

Sam Siciliano

A mysterious gypsy places a cruel curse on the guests at a ball. When a series of
terrible misfortunes affect those who attended the ball, Mr. Donald Wheelwright
engages Sherlock Holmes to find out what really happened that night. With the help
of his cousin Dr. Henry Vernier and his wife Michelle, Holmes endeavors to save
Wheelwright and his beautiful wife Violet from the devastating curse.

ISBN: 9780857686985

AVAILABLE JANUARY 2012

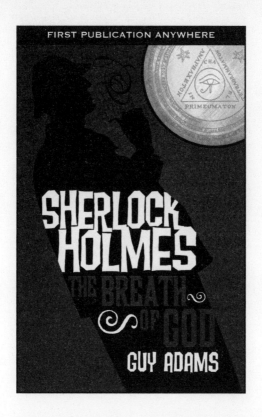

FIRST PUBLICATION ANYWHERE

SHERLOCK HOLMES
THE BREATH OF GOD

GUY ADAMS

THE FURTHER ADVENTURES
OF SHERLOCK HOLMES

THE BREATH OF GOD

Guy Adams

A body is found crushed to death in the London snow. There are no footprints
anywhere near. It is almost as if the man was killed by the air itself. This is the first
in a series of attacks that sees a handful of London's most prominent occultists
murdered. While pursuing the case, Holmes and Watson have to travel to Scotland
to meet with the one person they have been told can help: Aleister Crowley.
ISBN: 9780857682826

AVAILABLE SEPTEMBER 2011

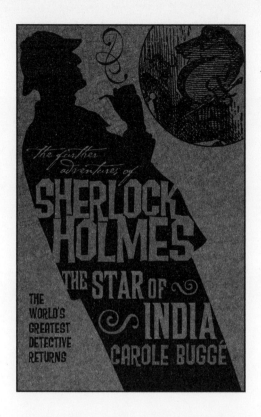

THE FURTHER ADVENTURES
OF SHERLOCK HOLMES

THE STAR OF INDIA

Carole Buggé

Holmes and Watson find themselves caught up in a complex chess board of a
problem, involving a clandestine love affair and the disappearance of a priceless
sapphire. Professor James Moriarty leads the duo on a chase through the dark and
dangerous back streets of London and beyond.

ISBN: 9780857681218

AVAILABLE AUGUST 2011

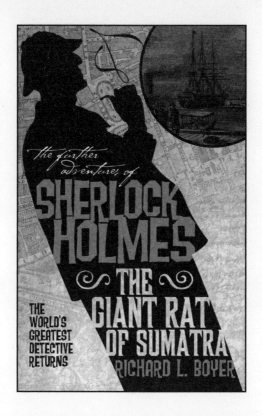

THE FURTHER ADVENTURES
OF SHERLOCK HOLMES

THE GIANT RAT OF SUMATRA

Richard L. Boyer

For many years, Dr. Watson kept the tale of The Giant Rat of Sumatra a secret.
However, before he died, he arranged that the strange story of the giant rat should
be held in the vaults of a London bank until all the protagonists were dead...
ISBN: 9781848568600

AVAILABLE NOW!

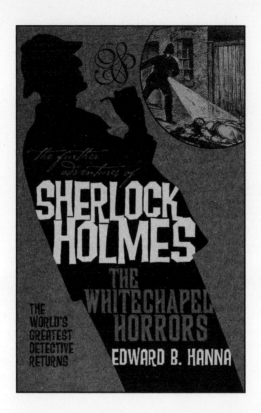

THE FURTHER ADVENTURES OF SHERLOCK HOLMES

THE WHITECHAPEL HORRORS

Edward B. Hanna

Grotesque murders are being committed on the streets of Whitechapel.
Sherlock Holmes believes he knows the identity of the killer–Jack the
Ripper. But as he delves deeper, Holmes realizes that revealing the
murderer puts much more at stake than just catching a killer…
ISBN: 9781848567498

AVAILABLE NOW!

THE FURTHER ADVENTURES
OF SHERLOCK HOLMES

DR. JEKYLL AND MR. HOLMES

Loren D. Estleman

When Sir Danvers Carew is brutally murdered, the Queen herself calls on
Sherlock Holmes to investigate. In the course of his enquiries, the esteemed
detective is struck by the strange link between the highly respectable Dr.
Henry Jekyll and the immoral, debauched Edward Hyde...

ISBN: 9781848567474

AVAILABLE NOW!

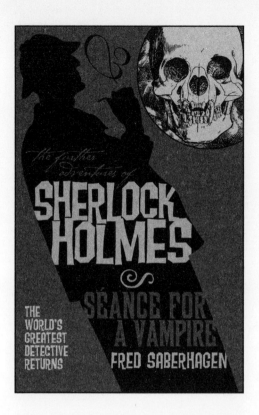

THE FURTHER ADVENTURES
OF SHERLOCK HOLMES

SÉANCE FOR A VAMPIRE

Fred Saberhagen

Wealthy British aristocrat Ambrose Altamont hires Sherlock Holmes
to expose two suspect psychics. During the ensuing séance, Altamont's
deceased daughter reappears as a vampire–and Holmes vanishes. Watson
has no choice but to summon the only one who might be able to help–
Holmes' vampire cousin, Prince Dracula.
ISBN: 9781848566774

AVAILABLE NOW!

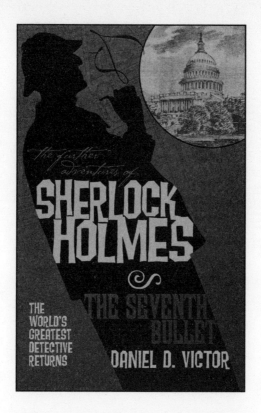

THE FURTHER ADVENTURES
OF SHERLOCK HOLMES

THE SEVENTH BULLET

Daniel D. Victor

Sherlock Holmes and Dr. Watson travel to New York City to
investigate the assassination of true-life muckraker and author
David Graham Phillips. They soon find themselves caught in a
web of deceit, violence and political intrigue, which only the great
Sherlock Holmes can unravel.
ISBN: 9781848566767

AVAILABLE NOW!

THE FURTHER ADVENTURES
OF SHERLOCK HOLMES

THE STALWART COMPANIONS

H. Paul Jeffers

Written by future President Theodore Roosevelt long before The
Great Detective's first encounter with Dr. Watson, Holmes visits
America to solve a most violent and despicable crime. A crime that
was to prove the most taxing of his brilliant career.
ISBN: 9781848565098

AVAILABLE NOW!

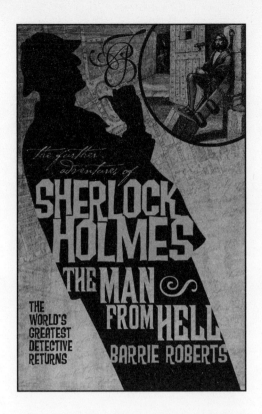

THE FURTHER ADVENTURES
OF SHERLOCK HOLMES

THE MAN FROM HELL

Barrie Roberts

In 1886, wealthy philanthropist Lord Backwater is found beaten
to death on the grounds of his estate. Sherlock Holmes and Dr.
Watson must pit their wits against a ruthless new enemy...
ISBN: 9781848565081

AVAILABLE NOW!

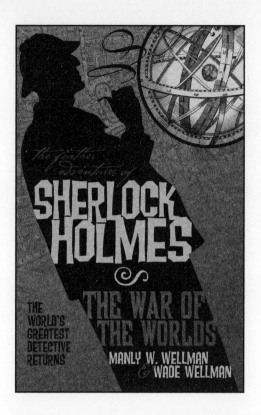

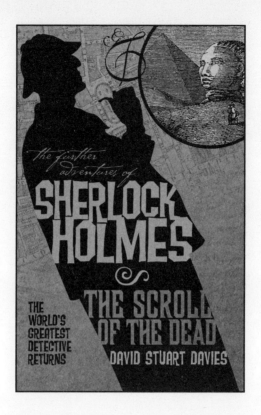

THE FURTHER ADVENTURES
OF SHERLOCK HOLMES

THE SCROLL OF THE DEAD

David Stuart Davies

Sherlock Holmes attends a séance to unmask an impostor posing
as a medium, Sebastian Melmoth, a man hell-bent on obtaining
immortality after the discovery of an ancient Egyptian papyrus. It
is up to Holmes and Watson to stop him and avert disaster.
ISBN: 9781848564930

AVAILABLE NOW!

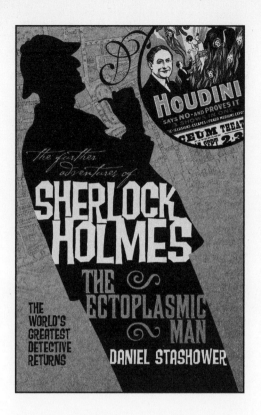

THE FURTHER ADVENTURES
OF SHERLOCK HOLMES
THE ECTOPLASMIC MAN

Daniel Stashower

When Harry Houdini is framed and jailed for espionage, Sherlock
Holmes vows to clear his name, with the two joining forces to take on
blackmailers who have targeted the Prince of Wales.

ISBN: 9781848564923

AVAILABLE NOW!

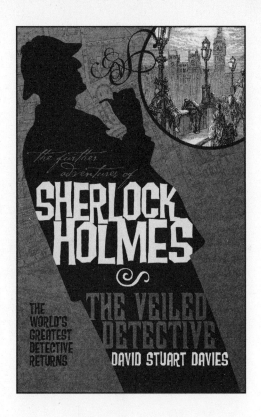

THE FURTHER ADVENTURES
OF SHERLOCK HOLMES

THE VEILED DETECTIVE

David Stuart Davies

A young Sherlock Holmes arrives in London to begin his career
as a private detective, catching the eye of the master criminal,
Professor James Moriarty. Enter Dr. Watson, newly returned
from Afghanistan, soon to make history as Holmes' companion...
ISBN: 9781848564909

AVAILABLE NOW!